The human heart has hidden treasures,

In secret kept, in silence sealed;

The thoughts, the hopes,
the dreams, the pleasures,

Whose charms were broken if revealed.

Charlotte Bronte

The heart's memory eliminates the bad and magnifies the good.

Gabriel Garcia Marquez

Perhaps the heart has a brain/mind that is insulated from the ravages of plaque in the demented brain.

Author

Second Time Around

Rebecca Graves

outskirts press

Second Time Around

v2.0

This is a work of fiction. Names, characters, businesses, places, events, locales, and incidents are either the products of the author's imagination or used in a fictitious manner. Any resemblance to actual persons, living or dead, or actual events is purely coincidental.

The opinions expressed in this manuscript are solely the opinions of the author and do not represent the opinions or thoughts of the publisher. The author has represented and warranted full ownership and/or legal right to publish all the materials in this book.

Outskirts Press, Inc.
http://www.outskirtspress.com

ISBN: 978-1-9772-3163-5

PRINTED IN THE UNITED STATES OF AMERICA

Chapter One

Cammy tightened the lid on the last jar of the dilly bean pickles. There! Twelve jars of beautiful tart green goodness lined up on her counter. She listened for the satisfying pop of the lids sealing as she cleaned up and put away her equipment. She had a little trouble lifting the large stainless steel canner to pour out the water, barely cool from sterilizing the jars. Water was so heavy, she thought, blocking out the annoying pain in her left wrist. Dean would be home soon and she needed to start dinner so they could be finished early enough for her to drive over to her dad's and supervise his bedtime routine.

Her dad still lived in the house Cammy and her sister had grown up in, on Magnolia Lane. At least, that's where they lived when Maggie was born. They had lived on Camellia when Cammy was born, both of the girls having been named after the street and the flower. (Susie was insistent that, in a time of naming girls Susan and Nancy and Barbara, her girls would have more distinctive names.) Bud was adamant that he did not want to leave his home. So far it was working well enough to have caregivers come in a couple of times a day and fix his meals, make sure he took his meds, and so on. Cammy's shift was bedtime. She lived closer, technically, to the sprawling ranch-style house on the southeast side of Memphis, as she was also south, just practically feet away from the Mississippi border. Being situated in the southwest corner of the state meant that Memphis had expanded east and north, but primarily east. Maggie lived way out in Collierville, which had once been a small sleepy town but was now part of greater Memphis. It was where the rich white people moved to after plain old east Memphis became too "diverse." Also they kept building bigger and bigger mansions, which required lots of space. Honestly, Cammy reflected as she drove, the mansions here these days. She remembered when they had considered Graceland a mansion. Ha! When she finally went there for the first time ever, just a few years ago, she had been shocked to see how relatively small it really was. Whenever she went out to Maggie's she saw dozens of places grander than that.

Maggie had married a cardiologist, a self-absorbed man happy to have Maggie work his way through medical school, only to ditch her in favor of his nurse once he opened his practice. But Maggie had hired a good lawyer and gotten a sweet deal in the divorce, including the big house and alimony. Now she didn't really have to work. She indulged her love of shopping in the guise of being a rare book finder. She went to garage sales, used bookshops, flea markets, Goodwill--any place that had books for sale--and snatched up ones that were on the collectible list. She could pay $.35 for a book at Goodwill and turn it around for a hundred bucks on the same day, if she got lucky. Once she had found, at an estate sale deep in the country, a first edition of *Lady Chatterley's Lover*, a volume that no self-respecting southern lady would own up to, and that no doubt had lain hidden in the attic for many years, which had fetched $10,000.

"How are you tonight, Bud?" Cammy greeted her father as she let herself in the back door. She had called him by his name ever since her parents' acrimonious divorce when she was twelve and Maggie was ten. The girls felt strongly that Bud was more to blame than Susie, their mother, but Susie just wanted out, and so she was the one to leave and give up everything, including custody of the girls. After that not much information came their way about what had really gone wrong with the marriage, so they were left with vague impressions and shadowy memories, in addition to the severe loss and abandonment issues. Because Susie had not just left, she had moved away, as far away as she could get, in the minds of the girls, although she was at least on the same continent. She had moved to Nova Scotia. But it might as well have been the moon, for all they saw of her. She sent birthday presents and Christmas presents and back-to-school shopping checks, and once a year, on her birthday, she allowed herself a long-distance phone call to each of the girls. Otherwise they had no contact with their mother.

"I'm starving," Bud replied weakly.

"What? Why are you starving? Didn't Esther make you dinner?"

"The supplies haven't come yet."

Oh. It was one of those nights.

"The Jerries took everything when they left, and our guys haven't come yet," was Bud's feeble response. He was time-traveling again, back in Germany, where his B-24 bomber had been shot down and he had been in a POW camp for three months at the end of the war.

Cammy looked around and saw a pot of soup on the stove, and a note from Esther that she had not been able to get him to eat anything. Esther was the dinnertime caregiver, who normally was able to charm Bud into doing the things he should do on her watch. Cammy knew it must be a bad night if Esther hadn't been able to manage it.

"Oh here they are now--whew! Just in time. And they brought this delicious soup! Here, have a bite," coaxed Cammy, holding a spoonful of lukewarm soup up to Bud's mouth. He opened his mouth but closed it again immediately.

"The news is our boys have won," he grumbled, "but

what the hell is taking them so long to get here?"

"Bud--they're here now--I just told you. See this nice soup they brought?" Cammy was trying hard not to let exasperation creep into her voice; Bud was astute as far as inflection and tone went, and it made him suspicious if he detected resentment or agitation. Then he was even more stubborn. She decided it was time to step back and take a new approach. "Oh well, that's okay, you don't have to eat if you don't want to. I'm sure the other guys will appreciate having more for themselves." Introducing the element of competition was brilliant; Cammy had to admire her skill there. Bud was ever alert for someone trying to get the jump on him.

"Let me try it then," he said, grabbing the spoon back from her. "Mm--it's a little on the cold side. But I guess it's better than nothing," was all he said about Esther's delicious navy bean soup with ham hock, as he devoured two bowls of it.

After that Cammy was able to get things back on track for Bud's bedtime routine, and she went home exhausted but satisfied. Still, she wondered, how long could things go on like this without ever more care?

Chapter Two

Maggie was just finishing her early morning yoga class when her phone went off. She had put it on vibrate but she could still hear it thrumming in her gym bag in the corner. Huh, she thought, who could be calling me this early? So she got up out of her sun salute, smiled apologetically at the teacher, and went to see who it was. No wonder it was early--the call was from Susie, her mother, from Nova Scotia, two or three time zones earlier, she never could remember which.

"Hello?" Maggie was mystified as to why her mother would be calling her, since it was not Susie's birthday. "Mama? What's up?" Susie would always be Mama to the girls, no matter how angry they were at her for leaving them.

"Oh hello dear--how are you? Did you get the check I sent for your back-to-school shopping? The first day of junior high is so important. I hope you got some fashionable things that flatter your figure."

Maggie felt a sinking sensation in her gut. Oh dear God, please don't let this be real. She had no idea how to even respond. Except she did, from her experience with her dad, whose dementia had been a fact of life for some time now. So she went with the tried and true.

"Yes we did, Mama. Thanks so much! Goldsmith's back-to-school sale was better than ever and I got some real nice things. How are you??"

"Oh I'm fine, I guess. It's just, I get lonely since Don passed away."

Just like that, she was back in real time. Maggie felt utterly confused. "I know Mama. Are you keeping busy? What about your sewing group--do you still go to that?"

"You know, the strangest thing happened last time I tried to go--I couldn't find it! It wasn't where it's always been. So I just went to the store and picked up some groceries instead."

"Hmm--that is strange. I wonder who we could ask about that to find out if they changed their location." Maggie was frantically looking through her contact list to see if she had any of her mother's friends listed. She only had two names--Don's children from a previous marriage. Susie had left her own two children, moved two thousand miles away, and gotten remarried to a widower with two children. Maggie's stepbrothers, as it were. She had met them once. She and Cammy had gone to their mother's wedding. They were thirteen and fifteen, the ages at which girls are the most insufferable and angry, and they were that and more. So no strong attachments were formed between the two sets of children, would be the most polite way to say it. The girls could not forgive Susie for starting a new life with different children. The husband they could forgive, but not the children.

In fact Don was a very nice man, a teacher at the school where Susie had found employment right away, having already been a teacher in Memphis for five years.

He taught third grade, and she got a job teaching

second grade, so they were thrown together from the start. To be fair, they did not marry immediately. They had a rather long courtship really--three years. His wife had died of breast cancer only a short time before the school year started, so he was grieving her for months before he felt ready to even talk to another woman in a friendly way (was their official story). He was nothing if not eminently likable, funny in a self-deprecating way, a staunch Catholic, and very kind.

How could it be true that Maggie had no names of her mother's friends up there? Did she even have friends? Maggie knew so little of Susie's life in Nova Scotia. Suddenly she was seized with such severe regret and sadness and longing that she had to sit down. The yoga class was breaking up by now and people were standing around in groups of two or three chatting.

"I don't know..." Susie was always vague about the people in her life. It was as if she didn't want to enthuse about Canada too much to her Memphis born and bred daughters, who stayed there their whole lives.

Another class started arriving to use the room--it was a Zumba class, which Maggie had tried once and almost had a heart attack. The teacher came in, saw Maggie, and gave her a delighted smile and thumbs up, thinking she had come to give it another go. Maggie shook her head, pointed to her phone, and began to gather up her things.

"Mama, let me call you back later, okay? I have to go now but I'll call you in a little while. Okay?"

"All right. I think I should be home. I mean, what else do I have to do?" Susie sounded so despondent that

Maggie was again seized with guilty remorse. She had to remind herself that Susie had made her choices and had to live with the consequences. Life is hard and then you die, was Maggie's basic outlook on life.

Cammy was draining the last drop from her second cup of strong coffee when Maggie called.

"I'm coming over. We have to talk!"

"Whoa, slow down! What's this about?" Cammy didn't care for surprises much. Not since the Big Surprise of her mother leaving their family came when Cammy was at the tender age of twelve, just when a girl needs her mother the most, even though she also had the developmental need to distance herself. Cammy had never been able to complete that cycle of rebel and reunify. She was stuck in resenting her mother forever, a sort of psycho-emotional purgatory really. And as far as surprises go, some would say that Cammy had become… well, a control freak. She did not like the feeling of something coming at her that she was not prepared for, so she went to great lengths to be prepared for anything and everything.

"Mama called me this morning," announced Maggie. That achieved the instant attention that Maggie knew it would.

"Okay, come over. But bring one of those cinnamon rolls from that bakery near the gym, and don't try to pretend that you didn't go there, because you always go there after yoga."

"I'll be there in twenty minutes."

Chapter Three

1921

A small steadfast town in Indiana. Florence lies panting on her bed in the sweltering room, attended by her mother and her sister. She is giving birth, although she is unmarried. The father's identity will remain forever undisclosed--a soldier that came through town on his way to ship out to the front, some would speculate. But there is no way to know. Florence will not name him or talk about it with anyone, except perhaps Mabel, her sister closest in age, and the other one who will remain forever a spinster with Florence. The other five sisters will all marry and have families, or they have already.

When confronted with her daughter's situation, Rachel, the mother of the seven, would not brook any discussion of going away to a home, or giving the baby up for adoption, or even having the child at a hospital. She had birthed all her girls at home and saw no reason Florence should not also. They would keep and raise the child. Period. No questions asked or answered. William, her husband, had no voice in the matter.

Thus did Bud Benson slide exuberantly out into the world.

He was cuddled, coddled, and spoiled by his mama, his aunties, and his grandmother. He had no given name other than Bud. At school he did get some raised eyebrows by the teachers, but he proved to be such an apt student and so very charming that they soon dropped that.

In high school Bud excelled in track and field and basketball. Being tall and handsome, he was very popular with the girls, plus he was an honor student. His ignominious beginnings were lost to success, and he suffered no lack of self-esteem. He could have gone to many different colleges but chose to enroll at Indiana University to stay close to home and his dear mama and Auntie Mabel and Grandma Rachel.

"Susie," Bud mutters to himself. He is time-traveling again, to chemistry class at IU. Susie was a very cute girl in the class, yes indeed. And always so smartly dressed.

"Oh, would you like me to help you with this assignment, Miss Susie?" he says to her one day.

"Why, I would so appreciate that, Mr. Buddy," came the saucy but sincere reply from Susie, who was secretly thrilled that this guy who looked a little like Clark Gable to her mind would speak to her.

"My name's Bud, not Buddy," came the slightly gruff response, while thinking, "This girl has some spirit."

"Oh, but I just like names ending in 'ie or y,'" she said with such a sweet smile that Bud was smitten instantly. "My father made me enroll in this chemistry class. I hate it and don't need it to graduate, but, as he reminds me every day, 'chemistry brings us a better standard of living,' or something to that effect. I fear I shall be a big disappointment to him by failing this course." And she looked at him so innocently and teasingly at the same time that he heard himself volunteering to help her by outside of class tutoring. And so it began.

It turned out that Susie's father was being quite literal in his pronouncement about the value of chemistry. It had been his ticket out of poverty, since he had been able to get a job at Eli Lilly with his chemistry degree, obtained by working nights and taking classes every day. He had worked hard and earned respect for it, and though it made him a rigid man, it brought material rewards.

Bud is lost in pleasant daydreams and memories when Esther comes to fix his dinner.

"How you doin' Mistah B?" She let herself in the back door.

"Oh come here girl, and let me kiss you till your teeth fall out!"

Esther recoils but then remembers the approach they have been trained in with dementia clients. (They have been instructed to refer to them as clients, not patients.)

He's on one of his trips, as she has come to think of them. And really, don't they say that time is not real, that everything exists at all times? Her grandson told her that, and he had learned it in physics class. She was not opposed to the idea, but she was still getting used to it. It was hard to picture. But Bud made it more visible to her in a way; the specificity of his lapses into other times made it seem like events of his life were out there somewhere, like a wax museum, just waiting to be reviewed or relived again and again.

"Ooh--no you don't! We ain't got time for that." Who

was that girl? Esther wondered. Bud must have been one sexy man.

"Susie, you cock-tease, come here!"

"You watch your language, Mister, or you might not get any for the next week!" This was probably going beyond the professional guidelines about patient/caregiver interactions, but Esther was sometimes forced to do that with Bud. He was a formidable challenge.

And it worked. Bud laughed, and that was like the snap of the magician's fingers that brings the hypnotized back to the present moment. "Esther!" he bellowed. "I'm starving---what's for dinner?"

Chapter Four

Susie felt so tired and defeated. She did not know what to do about her situation, which she had in lucid moments perceived accurately. I mean, who was she kidding about her sewing meeting not being where it always was? Come on. The truth was she got lost and disoriented and had no idea where she was. In a town she had lived in for decades. She was always one to see to the heart of any situation, and not one to mince words about it, usually.

She had friends here, to be sure. She and Don had made many close friendships over the years. People liked her--she was witty and smart to his put-on self-deprecating and bumbling humor. And of course the fact that they were both teachers made them beloved in their spheres. But people who like you are not necessarily able to be there for you when you really need them, she had noticed. Now that she was widowed, she got called less frequently to go out and do interesting things. And too, they were all getting older, and everyone had their problems and difficulties, or had just outright died already. So she could hardly lean on any of them and basically say "And oh by the way, I have a terrible degenerative brain disease, could you take care of me for the rest of my life?"

There were her stepsons, of course. With their attendant families. Tedious, if she were brutally honest. They had never really bonded, Susie and Ted and Michael. She of course carried massive loads of guilt for leaving her own two children, and the boys were grieving their own dead mother. So it would have been miraculous if they had bonded, was the way Susie always rationalized it to herself. But really would it have, she sometimes wondered. Because, again brutal honesty, she found them dull. They had no interest in books (and how could that happen in a teacher's home, one might ask). Or art, or music, other than the dreadful stuff teenagers listened to. Here they were, living very near the fabulous city of Halifax, home to some of the greatest music venues anywhere, including art museums, theatre, radio, and television, but all they wanted to do was hockey. Play hockey, watch hockey, talk about hockey endlessly, play fantasy hockey. If it was hockey related, you could bet Ted and Michael were into it. And naturally they had found wives who were also into it, and they had children that dutifully followed them down that path. Save for one delightful little girl--Flower. That was Susie's favorite grandchild. She was six, and a magical little sprite she was. Susie felt it was a shame for her to have been born to Ted, but there was nothing to do about it except try to introduce her to some of the finer things in life. She did that as much as she could, without seeming to favor one grandchild over another. It was tricky.

She had, briefly, entertained the notion of ending it all before it got ugly. I mean, people do that nowadays, she's seen it on the news. Just be buried next to Don and be out of everyone's way. That possibility was nipped in the bud when she realized that she could not be buried next to Don because their marriage was never recognized by the church, since she was divorced. She went to church with Don but was never allowed to partake of communion or any other ceremony. And now she is barred from the cemetery.

So no, Susie really felt she had no one to turn to in the end, for her own end, now terrifyingly imaginable to her, no one but her own flesh and blood family. Which is why she had called Maggie the other day, to bring up the exceedingly delicate idea of moving back to Memphis. But then when she had her on the phone, her damned mind started wandering and she must have said something completely inappropriate, though she had no memory of what it was. And then Maggie had to go and said she would call her back, but so far she had not. God knows what she thinks now, thought Susie.

Maggie was the one she had called because it was she whom Susie felt she got along with the best. Somehow she and Cammy had never come to terms, never got past the condition of distant, superficial affection. When Susie left, Maggie was young enough to wail and cry and ask why why why. And somehow Susie had been able to explain it to Maggie in a way that her open little mind could accept. ("It's like when you have a sliver in your finger and you have to get it out. It hurts, sometimes getting a sliver out hurts a lot. Or ripping a bandaid off of a scab--you know how much that hurts, right? But it has to be done. So that's what I can explain--I just have to do it.") Cammy, being twelve, was already past that.

And Maggie, as an adult, had actually, unbeknownst to Cammy, gone to Nova Scotia to visit Susie a couple of times. Once when her husband left her and she was in emotional distress, Susie had been able to comfort and console her and just love her up, which was so very satisfying to both of them. Susie regretted that Maggie had never had children, because then she, Susie, would have had her own grandchildren. Technically she had grandchildren, because Cammy had kids, but again, the distantness--she barely knew them. Cammy was the one with the stable marriage and children; she had lots to do, Susie supposed. And a career as a nurse to boot. Maggie had, after the cardiologist, only a series of love affairs that Susie had long since given up on keeping track of.

Susie dreams. In one dream there is Maggie, flitting like a butterfly from lover to lover while a handsome man looks on from a distance. In another, she herself is in a passionate embrace with a mystery lover, from which she awakens panting and aroused, and with a visceral sense of the color blue.

Chapter Five

It was true, Cammy had the stable marriage and a career and kids. Of course now she had retired from her nursing job at Methodist Hospital, where she had been a labor and delivery nurse for twenty-five years. She was worn out after that long, and had put in for a desk position, but then Dean got cancer, and she had to take care of him for a couple of years before he got back on his feet. After that, she just didn't feel like returning to work. She took up quilting instead. The walls of her home were covered with gorgeous quilts she had made, in every color of the rainbow .She found it very soothing; it was an arena in which you had total control, as opposed to labor and delivery, where anything might happen. One of her quilts had even won a ribbon at the Mid-South Fair, for best original design. She was very proud of that.

She was bent over a particularly difficult bit of piecework when Maggie rapped twice on the door and then let herself in, as was her habit. Cammy glanced at her to ascertain whether she had a bakery bag, and when she saw it, she put aside her handwork and greeted her sister with a brief hug.

"Coffee?" she asked.

"Oh yeah," replied Maggie. "Maybe a fresh pot."

"That bad, huh? What's going on? How come Mama called you?" Cammy had long since realized and accepted that Maggie was the one to communicate with Susie most of the time.

"Cam--you won't believe it. Here's what she said: 'Did you get the check I sent for your back-to-school shopping? The first day of junior high is so important. I hope you got something flattering to your figure.'"

Cammy chuckled. "Still harping about your weight. She'll never let that go, will she?" Maggie was the more zaftig of the two of them, and had battled that her whole life.

"Cammy! JUNIOR HIGH! She's time-traveling! She has dementia now!"

Cammy paused in mid-bite of her cinnamon roll. She had not really focused in on that part of the statement, had just thought Maggie was complaining about her mother's preoccupation with her fat issue. "Oh Lord, no!" The implications of that were immediately apparent to her. The sisters just stared at each other for a long minute, each one knowing every thought they were simultaneously having. How would they deal with this from two thousand miles away? Who could possibly take care of their mother? And, in the recesses of their minds, the worry that if both of their parents had dementia, weren't they themselves liable to get it?

"But then--in the next second, she was back to reality, saying she was lonely and missed Don. So I don't know, maybe it was just a momentary glitch or something. Does dementia even work that way? But also she said she had tried to go to her sewing group the other day and it wasn't there, she couldn't find it. And I don't even have a single name of any of her friends to call and ask about her. The only names I have are Ted and Michael, who probably haven't even noticed anything because, well just because. You know how they are."

"We don't really, other than what we've heard from Susie. But I suppose we can trust her on that one," Cammy said, chewing thoughtfully. "Still, we could call them. Especially since they're the only contacts we have up there other than her. What choice do we have?"

Maggie agreed with a dip of her head as she took a sip of her coffee. "Should we do it right now? I mean, there's nothing to be gained by procrastinating, is there?" Maggie had inherited that gene from Susie, the quick decision-making, whereas Cammy, with her need for control, was more deliberate.

"I guess we could, but it doesn't seem like an emergency yet, does it? Not that we should wait until it is one, but she did sound partly sane, right? Maybe they will call us first. I say we hold off a bit."

Maggie shrugged and took another bite of cinnamon roll. Privately she was entertaining the notion of making a quick trip up to Nova Scotia to see for herself. But she said nothing of this to her sister.

Chapter Six
1948

Bud is graduating from Indiana University with a Bachelor of Science degree in chemistry. He is back from the war, where he spent what would have been his last two years in college in training with the Army Air Corps, practicing and flying raids in a B-24 bomber, until his plane was shot down over Germany three months before the Allies prevailed over Hitler. He gazes around the stadium, where the guests are seated. There are all his proud family members--Florence, Mabel, Grandma Rachel, and assorted cousins and old friends. It has felt like a dream to him, being back here, going on with classes, as if nothing had changed. He had plowed himself into school after spending the summer recovering from the POW camp, and finished early by doing summer sessions the following summer. And now graduation! He looks at Susie, beautiful Susie, who had graduated two years before, when he would have too if he had not gone to war. She beams at him adoringly, and suddenly he feels alive again. Truly we did live in the best country! Anything was possible.

Bud couldn't think how he had made it through those two years without Susie. He had carried her picture next to his heart every day, and even though his plane was shot down and he ended up in a POW camp in Germany with none of his possessions, he still had that. It sustained him through times of hunger and cold, through fear and despair and horror. Looking at that bright smiling face, her sweet lips and sharp eyes, brought joy when there was nothing else. And now here she was, his very own. She had waited patiently for him when she didn't know if he was dead or alive. He felt he was the luckiest man on earth. They were to be married the next day! And miraculously, she was still a virgin! That last night before he shipped out it had been dicey. But Bud was damned if he would spawn a bastard child as his own father had done, and then go off to war, perhaps never to return. Susie did not have the family support that Florence had. She came from a well-to-do family in Indianapolis, with parents so emotionally distant that the most affection they had ever shown him was a cool handshake the night before he left for the front, even though he and Susie had been together for two years.

Bud is not particularly looking forward to the actual wedding itself, as it had been planned by Susie's aspirational mother as a full-out Catholic church wedding, with all the accompanying parties, announcements, invitations, rituals, ceremonies, and what-have-you. This very night after graduation they had to drive up to Indianapolis for the rehearsal dinner. He comes from a more casual, small town church, where all the hoopla is a little too much. They might have a rehearsal dinner, but it would be a picnic in the backyard, for example. No, what he was excited about was the actual living with Susie, day after day. He was entranced by her--her quick wit, the good-girl looks she wore over a slightly bad-girl tendency. And not bad really, just an adventure-loving, risk-taking side to her that is tantalizing to him. Especially since he has been in the war, out in the world. He's seen a few things. Heard a few things.

They would be moving to Tennessee after spending their honeymoon at The Dells in Wisconsin. They didn't have much money, but at least Susie's family was footing that bill, along with the wedding. After all, that was the bride's parents' job, wasn't it? And they would stay in Bud's hometown for a week, to say goodbye to all his relatives. But then pack up all their worldly belongings and begin a whole new life that was just their life! He and Susie! He can hardly stand the excitement and anticipation of it.

He has gotten a job right off the bat with Wonder Bread, which had recently figured out how to enhance its product with 12 vitamins and minerals, and he would be overseeing that process at their plant in Memphis. Of course Wonder Bread was a product integral to Bud's life, and indeed most everyone, having been the first baking company to introduce bread in the package already sliced. Hence the popular phrase "better than sliced bread," because sliced bread had just been the bees' knees for an entire country. Also the sheer pure whiteness of it, and the fact that it was a 1.5 pound loaf instead of the traditional one pounder made it the most popular bread on the shelves. Bud was proud to work for such a company. Despite Bud's assurances that his salary would be more than sufficient, Susie had applied for a job with the city schools, having earned a BS in Elementary Education, and then taught for two years while Bud finished his degree. She expected to continue her career, and just ignored his insistence that they would not need her income. Yes, she thought happily, everything was looking very rosy indeed.

Chapter Seven

1952

Susie remembers sleep. Fondly. She had once been such a great sleeper, as a child and a teenager. It was one of her favorite things. But apparently the human female is designed to let that go after giving birth to a child. Because she has become a lighter-than-air sleeper, alert to every little murmur and movement by her baby, actually now two babies. That plus the bottles. The doctor had told her that her milk was "too thin" and that she should just bottle feed, so, not knowing any better, she did. That meant getting up every two hours or three or four, however many Cammy decided to allow her on any given night, and heating up the milk to just the right wrist-tested temperature, and sitting in the rocker in the living room so as not to disturb Bud and feeding her baby. Then tiptoeing back into the bedroom, returning Cammy to her crib, and crawling into bed beside Bud, who invariably would sigh, roll over to her side, and drape his arm over her. Susie has learned something about herself that she had no reason to know before sharing a bed with a husband. She really cannot sleep with someone's arm draped over her. Having grown up in a household of non-touchers, she wasn't at all used to touch. I mean, who knew touch was something one could be so sensitive to? She had been so eager to finally sleep with Bud.

The almost animal magnetism that they felt for each other was strong, but when the sex part was over, she found she just wanted to roll away and get in a fetal position on her side, put her hand under her cheek, and drift off to dreamland. Bud, on the other hand, wallowed in the long after-glow of sex. He could fall asleep in the blink of an eye, and frequently did, lying atop her in blissful abandon while she felt him grow ever heavier on her slight frame.

And then there was Maggie, so the whole thing started all over again. Even though Maggie is nearly one and a half now, she still doesn't sleep through the night. She has never been an "easy" baby. On the rare days when Cammy's nap coincides with Maggie's, Susie can sleep in the afternoon. At least enough to look and feel presentable when her husband gets home from work, although the housework suffers from this system. Bud is pretty forgiving on this score, but sometimes she can detect a slight eyebrow raising at the piles of clean laundry on the couch, or the late dinner hour.

Her dreams of teaching have been put on hold, since she turned up pregnant almost immediately after they got settled in Memphis, in a little one-bedroom bungalow on Camellia, out almost to the eastern city limit, which was Highland Avenue at the time. They hadn't really thought about their family growing so fast, had thought that the little place would hold them for a while, but when Maggie was conceived only seventeen months after Cammy was born, they realized they needed to find a bigger place right away. Moving, with a toddler and while pregnant, in the stifling heat and humidity of the mid-south had been a form of torture for Susie, who had been shielded from any such real-life hard tasks her whole life. But she loves their new home, a generous-sized rambler beyond the city limit, out almost to the little town of White Station, which there is talk of annexing as part of the city. It is on Magnolia Lane, a winding shady road with stately oaks and real magnolia trees. It is the best place Susie has ever lived. There is a screened-in back porch with a hanging two-person swing! If there is a cooling breeze blowing through, it's lovely to sit out there with her babies, rocking and reading.

Bud is advancing nicely in his career. It's just as well, he realizes, that he couldn't go back to serve in the army in Korea, though that was his inclination. Due to being a veteran already, and the hardship his dependents (now three!) would have to bear, he got an exemption from the draft and is now immersed in business. He has gotten involved with more than just the chemistry aspect of Wonder Bread, having been perceived as someone with ideas, up-and-comingness, and all that. Bud has made sure to take advantage of his good job and shining prospects by reaping some rewards, in the form of material possessions. There was a fairly new invention, one that not many ordinary people had yet, called television, that he had been hell-bent on getting. And so they had purchased one straight away, as soon as they got to Memphis and moved into the bungalow on Camellia. It was delivered two weeks before Cammy was born in '49. "I mean, jeez--it's been on the market for ten years already," rationalized Bud. He got no argument from Susie--her parents had gotten one back in '44, and she rather liked it.

Anyway, one day he was watching television while feeding Cammy (that was at least one advantage of bottle feeding--Daddy can share the job), and saw a brand new show called The Howdy Doody Show. A guy named Buffalo Bob (one Bob Smith from Buffalo) had a red-haired, freckled marionette dressed like a cowboy that was Howdy. Various additional personae--Princess SummerFallWinterSpring, Phineas T. Bluster, and Clarabell the Clown, along with many others--made up the large cast of characters on the show. Bud saw immediately that this was going to be a popular show, and hit upon the brilliant idea of enlisting Wonder Bread as a sponsor of it. He was so enthusiastic about it that the bosses in the marketing department were won over easily. The company had enjoyed instant success with the advertising campaign--their bold primary colors on pure white wrappers went perfectly with the colors of Howdy Doody. And parents like the "Builds Strong Bodies Eight Ways" slogan. Wonder Bread loaves flew off the shelves, Wonder Bread's stock shot up in value, and Bud got a big raise. That's how they could afford the rambler-style house on Magnolia. It was all due to Howdy Doody. And now Bud was the new wonder boy in the marketing department. He was in demand, even had a few other companies seeking him out now and then. Wining and dining him. They always included Susie at first, and she liked being taken out to dinner, but with the two babies, it was hard to arrange a babysitter and get all dressed up when she was just so exhausted all the time. She didn't mind if Bud went alone. Sometimes he brought back portions for her--uneaten bits, or an extra dessert.

Chapter Eight

Maggie was having a field day. She had been driving around out in the country, just exploring, stopping at little corner stores to get beer and cheese and other snacks, when she came across the messiest junk store she had ever seen, in the "town" of Rossville. It was a dusty old barn so densely packed with stuff that there was barely room to squeeze through the narrow aisles between shelves and tables piled high with treasures. More stuff hung from the ceiling, bigger items were outside--it seemed to go on forever. Good thing she had stopped for provisions--she could happily waste a whole day here.

Finally she found what she was looking for--the bookshelf that you had to ask the man to open. And BINGO--there it was--a first printing of *Lonesome Dove* by Larry McMurtry, just waiting to be discovered by some lucky person who knew what they were looking at. It wouldn't bring in that much--only about $350, but still, a first edition that was in pristine condition was pretty rare. She had to practically beg to purchase it from the proprietor--a grumpy and grizzled curmudgeon that seemed not to want to sell any of the thousands of items he had on display. In the end he agreed to take $25 for it, and probably secretly thought he had gotten the best of her. She dug a Wet Wipe out of her purse to clean her fingers of greasy cheese before taking it from the old man.

"Could I have a bag please?" she asked.

"It's just one lousy book--can't you carry it?" he growled.

"I don't want it to get dirty. My car is not the cleanest in the world." Inwardly Maggie rolled her eyes. "Or maybe wrap it in some brown paper."

The shopkeeper sighed, bent down below the counter, and grudgingly handed her a brown paper grocery bag. Maggie placed the book in the bag and folded the excess around it.

"Thank you," she trilled as she threaded her way back toward the entrance.

She was in such a good mood that she opened the sunroof on her BMW and decided to stop for one more beer on her way home. It was a beautiful Indian summer day--not a cloud in the sky, temperature about 75, and a slight breeze blowing. When her phone rang, she just answered it without checking to see who it was first. It was Susie.

"Oh Mama! Oh my gosh, I just realized I never did call you back the other day! I'm so sorry!"

"Did you know I was anemic? All those years I was so tired? It turned out I was anemic."

Maggie wasn't sure what was happening here. Was Susie time-traveling again? "Um, no, I guess I never knew that, Mama."

"Well, I was. My doctor never even checked for that. Although thankfully he did at least offer me some birth control. I mean I just couldn't face having another baby with the two of you girls already."

"I can understand that. I do vaguely remember you being tired a lot."

"I remember that doctor visit like it was yesterday. He hemmed and hawed and asked me how many children I planned on having. I must have looked surprised, because he then asked what I knew about birth control. And I knew zero. Because my mother never once talked to me about any of that stuff. When she had 'the birds and bees' talk with me, it was so devoid of any anatomical information, or any hint that it could be pleasurable, that I actually thought you had to go to a clinic or hospital to conceive. Can you believe that? But then, you never really knew my mother."

Maggie was thinking, yeah, then you left us before me or Cammy started our periods and made Dad handle all of that, so how was that any better? But all she said was, "So what did the doctor give you?" She was becoming increasingly uncomfortable with this conversation.

"Marriage hygiene, they called it back in those days. He did an exam and measured my cervix and gave me a diaphragm. Bud preferred that to the rubbers we sometimes used. He used to say that was like taking a shower with boots on!" and she let out a barky laugh.

Okay, TMI, Maggie was thinking. She tried to change the subject. "Um, Mama, what were you calling about?"

There was a pause, and then Maggie heard her take a deep breath. "I'm calling to say something that may shock you. I'm wishing now that I hadn't... I mean, if I had just not been anemic... it wasn't so terrible... Dammit, I could have grown old there and had grandchildren and not found myself all alone in this godforsaken place!" There--she had said it.

Maggie's thoughts evaporated, leaving nothing in her brain except roiling emotions. "Um, wow. I mean, what do you expect me to say to that, Mama?" she asked. "Are you saying you regret the last five decades of your life??"

"Here's what I was thinking," Susie continued without answering Maggie's question. "Wait, first of all, how is Bud doing?"

"Let's see, he definitely has times of clarity but then his mind starts wandering, time-traveling, as we think of it. We have a couple of caregivers come in and fix his meals, and then we do the bedtime shift." Of course by 'we' she meant Cammy, since it was her 99% of the time. "He insists on staying in the house though." She felt like adding "Is that what's happening to you too?" but refrained.

"And what is the house like these days?"

"Same as it always was." Exactly the same, she was thinking, as the day you left. It was as if it were a shrine. Bud had not wanted anything to change, presumably in case Susie should change her mind and come back. It was mired in the mid-century decor and color schemes--the rusts and chartreuses and ambers, the Danish Modern furniture--and suddenly Maggie saw clearly how shabby it was looking.

"What? What do you mean--exactly the same?" Susie could not grasp the idea of Bud not keeping up with design trends and fashions.

"I mean just that--not one thing has changed in the

house since you left." Somehow this had never come up before.

Now it was Susie's turn to be left speechless. All these years she had assumed that Bud, who was so eager to be on the cutting edge, would have kept up with the times. The pause hung heavily between them. The weight of what she had done so long ago came crashing down on her soul, and she sent up a prayer to heaven for forgiveness.

"Oh honey," was all she could say.

Chapter Nine

Cammy was cursing under her breath as she pawed through the box in a dark, hard-to-reach lower cupboard that contained the lids to her motley assortment of plastic containers. Why, and how in God's name, were there no matching sets, despite her having purchased such sets many times over the years? Sighing mightily, she strapped a large rubber band around a bottom and a lid that could not have been more than two millimeters off from fitting exactly. What the hell? Was it just her maybe? Was she getting old enough to lose fine motor skills or what?

She put away the leftover meatloaf and got her jacket out of the hall closet. It was beginning to look like rain, even though it was still sweltering hot. On second thought, she put the jacket back and just got out an umbrella. Maybe it would hold off until after she got back from Bud's, but better to be prepared just in case.

On the drive over to Magnolia Lane, Cammy remembered nostalgically the days of her youth, when there was only Tupperware. Susie had gone to her fair share of Tupperware parties and hosted some too, so there was a supply of every size and shape container you could possibly need, with no mistaking the lids. She thought fondly of Mrs. Wise, the girls' babysitter after Susie left, who would make huge pots of stews and soups for Bud and the girls to work on, so that he wouldn't have to cook when he got home from work. Oh he could cook, and sometimes he wanted to grill out or make something special, so they didn't always dine on Mrs. Wise's food, but it was reassuring to look into the refrigerator and see several large vessels of food ready to eat. She should just take some of those old containers home with her, she thought. Esther didn't need to use them for just Bud--he didn't even eat that much anymore.

Dear Mrs. Wise. She sometimes stayed with them for days at a time when Bud went out of town on business. It was almost like having a grandmother. Of course they had two grandmothers but they were both in Indiana, and were rarely seen--or in the case of Susie's mom, never, after Susie left. Mrs. Wise let them have choices about what they wanted for dinner, she helped them with their homework, folded their laundry, let them watch TV, read to them, and tucked them into bed, although Cammy felt she was too old for that.

As she pulled into the driveway, Cammy was surprised to see Maggie's car already parked there. This was highly unusual. What was going on? She quickly got out and let herself in the front door. Maggie was standing in the living room, hands on her hips, just looking around.

"Look at this," Maggie said with no greeting at all. "Nothing has changed here for fifty years! Not one single thing! How is that possible?"

"Um, I guess nobody wanted anything to be different," replied Cammy, who felt that Maggie's tone had been slightly accusatory, as if it was somehow her fault. "And why are you suddenly here noticing this for the first time?"

Maggie gave her sister a look and said, "Brace yourself. You might want to sit down to hear this." They sank into the olive green couch that was still in very good shape, due to the custom of southerners not using the living room. Most of the wear and tear had happened in the den.

"Mama called me again today. The other day when she called--remember I told you--I was supposed to call her back but I forgot. Anyway, she called me and she really seemed quite sound of mind. She said--are you ready for this? She said basically that she regrets what she did and wishes she had never left. She actually said, 'Dammit, I could have grown old there and had grandchildren and not found myself all alone in this godforsaken place!'"

"What?!?! How exactly did she broach that subject??"

"And she asked about the house, and Daddy." Bud was still Daddy to Maggie. "When I told her the house was exactly the same, she was stunned. Shaken really, was my impression. You know how they both were about keeping up with trends and fashions. I got the feeling that she had been about to ask another question but was so sad about the house that she couldn't go on. That's why I came here, to give you the update in person."

"Well, fuck me. Pardon my French. What are we supposed to do with that??"

"She blamed it all on her being anemic, and being so tired all the time," Maggie continued. "And then she started giving me way too much information about their sex life...."

"WHAT?!?!?" Cammy felt like shaking Maggie.

"It kind of ruined my day. I was having the best day--I found the most amazing junk store and scored a first edition of *Lonesome Dove*--"

"Mags! Focus! I don't care about your day! I want to know about Susie!"

"Camellia? Is that you?" Bud's rickety voice jiggled into the living room, the volume of their conversation having risen to a level that his ears could detect from the back of the house. "Is someone with you?"

The daughters looked at each other and turned to go to him.

"Hi Bud--look who showed up! Your other daughter!" Cammy's implied slur was not lost on her sister.

Chapter Ten
1953

The company that has won Bud's heart and replaced Wonder Bread as his employer (although he is still on good terms with everyone there, and especially maintains ties with the Howdy Doody Show people) is Holiday Inn, a new enterprise started by Memphian Kemmons Wilson after a family vacation to Washington, D.C., disappointed him in terms of lodging. The first motel had opened just the previous August. And now with Bud on board, three more were set to open on some of the main highways ushering travelers into Memphis. Bud helped shape the company mission statement really, which was that their inns be standardized, clean, predictable, family-friendly, and readily accessible. And now he was working on the Great Sign, as it was being called, the giant neon, instantly recognizable green sign with the golden arrow that would be the hallmark of all Holiday Inns across America.

It was very expensive but Bud convinced the powers that be that it would be worth it in the long run. So these days he was traveling to different states and spreading the Holiday Inn gospel far and wide.

Susie finds, to her surprise, that after the initial dismay of having her husband gone for two to five days at a time, she doesn't mind it so much. She is actually able to sleep, now that Cammy is four and Maggie is sleeping through the night (Susie has read her Dr. Spock), and no one has his arm draped across her. Then she has energy to be with them all day. She has even bought a sewing machine and is teaching herself to sew, although with Bud's increasing prosperity they can afford anything they want. She takes advantage of the girls' nap time to sew, having discovered she likes the productive feeling of creating something and then seeing her adorable toddler wearing it in public.

And really, Maggie is the darlingest little thing you ever saw. A redhead! Where that came from is anyone's guess, though with the Scotch-Irish-English ancestry of both Susie and Bud, it's not that surprising. Viking descendants were everywhere. She has the redhead temperament too--slightly volatile and mercurial, but Cammy is a moderating influence on her, even acting in the mother capacity when Susie's attention might be elsewhere momentarily.

Another thing Susie has discovered: she likes cooking. Before she was married, she had never so much as boiled water (the two years she taught while waiting for Bud, she had moved back home and lived with her parents again). And then with the babies coming right away, and this, that, and the other thing, she was embarrassed to realize that Bud did a lot of the cooking. Having been raised by a household of women, he had learned a lot in that department. The meals she did manage to make were pretty basic meat and potatoes type stuff, which is all she ever was exposed to in her parents' home. But now she is experimenting with bolder dishes, like lasagna and casseroles. She has scratched out a little herb garden in the side yard and is attempting to grow some parsley and oregano and sage. She takes the girls to the local library over on Highland and looks at cookbooks while Cammy chooses books she wants to check out and Maggie takes books off the shelves and throws them on the floor until the librarian comes over and gives Susie the evil eye. Then Susie tells Cammy to put them back where they go, which she does, the little angel. Cammy is the serious one, the rule follower.

Susie acquires another new gadget--a transistor radio, which she earned through redeeming her S&H Green Stamps--fifteen books of stamps, it cost. She plays it while she's cooking, singing along to Hank Williams' "Your Cheatin' Heart" and stirring her spaghetti sauce.

Chapter Eleven

The call, which they were not really expecting, came sooner than they had thought it might, if it did. Maggie's phone rang early one Saturday morning as she was getting ready to go to the Flea Market down at the fairgrounds, an activity she always looked forward to. Sometimes she got lucky there and came home with a book or two, but if that didn't happen she usually picked up some little treasure or other that made her happy anyway. She didn't recognize the number but saw that it was from Canada.

"Hello?" she asked, apprehension creeping into her consciousness like water seeping under a doorway.

"Hello Maggie? It's Ted. From Nova Scotia." He cleared his throat. "I know you must be wondering why I'm calling, so let me just say it's probably nothing, okay? Don't freak out."

Maggie rolled her eyes. Way to engender confidence that it's nothing, she thought. He might as well have accompanied the call with bombshell emojis and danger sign GIFs. "What is it, Ted? What's going on?"

"Okay, you might be aware that we do check in on Mo--... your mom regularly. I mean she is the grandmother to our kids."

"Yes sure, I know. Go on."

"So, the other day Mick dropped in, and she was

acting kinda strange. She was making a list of places she could hide things in the house."

"What do you mean? What kinds of things?"

"Appeared to be just little things, like no bigger than a slip of paper. She had places listed like the back of a shelf in the pantry, and the inside of the flour canister lid. When Mick asked her about it, she said, 'I want him to remember my face.' Mick said, 'Who?' and she just said, 'Why, Bud of course.' So that's when Mick figured she was lost in time."

"Have you guys ever noticed this before? Because I have lately, and we've been wondering what's happening up there. We had planned to call you but then… um, we just never did."

"We didn't want to say anything until we felt sure, but yeah, she's been weird lately. Like sometimes a dreamy look comes over her and she starts having, like, a conversation with an imaginary person. Or sometimes, she seems perfectly normal but then she'll ask about someone who's been dead for years. Like that."

Maggie sighed. "I don't suppose you have any ideas for what to do with her?" she asked Ted. "We don't have the slightest clue about her life up there really. Are there good assisted living places, and are they affordable, or what? And what is her financial situation exactly?" This was especially something the girls worried about when they talked about Susie.

Ted cleared his throat again. "Well, that's the other thing we've been meaning to call you about. She's uh… she's been sending money orders to some people.

Actually quite a few."

"What do you mean? What people? She hasn't sent any to us."

"No, it's strangers. She just doesn't think they're strangers. She thinks they're her friends. These Jamaicans call her up and tell her stuff like she's won the Australian Lottery for four million dollars but she just needs to pay the taxes before they can release the money to her."

"WHAT?!?!?" Maggie shrieked.

Ted rushed on, as if once he had started, he had to tell it all before he lost courage. "Yeah, the bank won't even let her draw out a money order anymore. They say it's a scam of some sort."

"Well DUH!" Maggie shouted into the phone. "When exactly did you decide this was a problem??? How much has she sent out?"

One more throat clearing. "She's sent out about $75,000, as near as we can figure. There's no way to know for sure though. They keep getting more and more clever about how she should send it. The last time they told her to send cash in the pages of a book. The bank alerted us when she withdrew two thousand in cash, and we were able to intercept that package thanks to a nice postal clerk who remembered her and still had the package in the outbound bin."

"Jesus Fucking Christ, Ted! And when did you think it might be a good idea to tell us this? Yesterday?"

"I know. Jeez, I'm sorry Maggie. I thought... we thought we could take care of it. We had her phone number changed and everything, but of course she has her cell phone, and she has all their numbers written on little scraps of paper all over the house, so she calls them too. There's this one guy she calls Tony, who she thinks is her friend, and who she thinks lives in Toronto, but he's actually in Jamaica, because we looked at the phone call record. There doesn't seem to be any official agency that has jurisdiction over international scams like this. We figure there might be a need to have an intervention."

"No shit, Sherlock. Sorry Ted, I know you were trying, but my God--this is serious. I'm coming up there. Maybe I'll bring Cammy too. I'll let you know details when I book flights."

"Okay. We'll try to keep close tabs on her till you get here."

"Is she even capable of caring for herself at this point?"

"Oh yes--that's the really strange part. She seems, or usually seems, perfectly fine. Drives, goes to church, goes to bridge club--all the stuff she does is still the same. It's just the Jamaican thing. Oh, and now the time-traveling thing."

"Huh," was all Maggie could manage to say. She felt a sudden urgency to get off the phone and start looking for flights. "Okay, thanks for calling me, Ted," though she had to bite her tongue to keep from adding 'finally.'

"That's the weirdest thing I ever heard of," Maggie said to herself after she and Ted had ended their call. She felt a strong urge to call Cammy, but hesitated. Should she burden her sister with all this? Or just go up there and straighten it out herself? Wouldn't it be hard to "straighten out"? It seemed to Maggie that it would require a major life change of some sort, for somebody. She hoped it wouldn't have to be her. Could she even conceive of going up there to that mysterious place so far away and living there?? No. Why would that even occur to her? That was crazy.

Chapter Twelve

In the end it was unthinkable that Maggie wouldn't tell Cammy about all of it. As soon as she thought about it seriously, she realized that was folly. They were allies in this fight, with all the history there. They needed to hammer out a plan. Brainstorm possibilities. Should she ask Cammy to go with her to Nova Scotia? Yes, that might be the best way. If she couldn't afford the ticket, Maggie would help her. That *Lonesome Dove* money might just do it. No, that probably wouldn't be enough; she would have to throw in that *Gone with the Wind* first edition in a dust jacket she had found at the flea market last time. Cammy and Dean had never been that financially secure, despite her having a nursing career. Dean was self-employed, a building sub-contractor who could do plumbing and electrical, which you might think would be lucrative, but somehow it was not. He was not good at the business and marketing end of things, and failed to keep up with going rates of pay, so that he was the cheapest but still somehow the most part-time person in the field. He was perhaps too nice. And ever since he had cancer (prostate, caught in time and dispatched), he felt he was entitled to be retired. Of course, self-employed people have to have saved up for their own retirement, which Dean never had the foresight or the extra money to do. Basically he had no retirement except Social Security, which was not enough to live on. Once in a while he did take on small jobs for friends, when there were extra expenses. Mainly they lived on Cammy's nursing pension, which was decent, but they still had to budget to be able to afford property taxes, insurance, and just the cost of living these days. Taking trips was a luxury they didn't often indulge in.

Maggie set to work looking for flights. It would be best if she went to Cammy's armed with all necessary details to convince her sister, whom she knew would be reticent. In her mind she was forming a vague plan that involved them going up there, taking things in hand, and finding Susie a nice assisted living place that would be very low cost. I mean, didn't Canada have socialized medicine, after all? Wasn't old-age care included in that?

Chapter Thirteen
1956

Susie is excited to start her job--finally! It was a long hard argument, but Bud has agreed that she can work outside the home now that Cammy is entering first grade and Maggie is in nursery school. Cammy's September birthday just squeaked under the cutoff date. So she will be one of the youngest in the class, but that's all right with Susie. Cammy is old for her age. Susie has secured a job in the very school that Cammy will be attending--their neighborhood school! It's almost too perfect to be believed. It's a new school, open only for two years, so that will be nice. Susie will be teaching fourth grade, just upstairs from Cammy's first-grade classroom.

The night before the first day, Cammy is so anxious and nervous that she cannot go to sleep, and Susie has to lie down with her and sing lullabies until she thinks she will nod off herself. But she cannot, because Bud is just home from a long trip and he will want to cuddle and so forth, and then too, she is as nervous as Cammy. She goes over and over her plan for tomorrow in her mind and begins to sing it instead of a lullaby. It's what finally puts Cammy to sleep. Susie gets up carefully and tiptoes out of the room the girls share and into her own room, where Bud is already in the bed, waiting expectantly for her. He hums one of their favorite songs, "Stardust" by

Hoagy Carmichael*, which Susie does still love of course, but she has also started liking the new sounds around town--Elvis Presley, Carl Perkins, LaVern Baker. She hasn't shared this with Bud so far. To be fair, it hasn't been that long, and he was gone quite a while this time--all the way to New York and Massachusetts. He came home all excited about something or other, but she was so preoccupied with planning what she would wear, and what the girls would wear, that she wasn't really paying close enough attention to what he was talking about. Something about Howdy Doody. She would simply fake remembering it when he talked about it again. Speaking of faking, she is going to have to exercise that womanly privilege tonight, since she cannot stop her mind from racing enough to concentrate on the sex. Because sex requires concentration on the woman's part, and perhaps on men's too. But when a man can't concentrate enough, it is revealed for all the world to see, or specifically just his partner. A woman has the great power to choose whether or not to admit to unfulfillment. This thought is also running through her mind even as she moans with exaggerated pleasure.

Fulfilled and spent, Bud at least does her the favor of rolling off of her before falling asleep. Susie gets up and goes to the bathroom for a little cleanup and to put some pin curls in her hair. When she climbs back in bed, she arranges herself comfortably on her side, and then Bud flops over, cups her left breast in his hand, and goes on sleeping. She can feel his hand, as warm as a heating pad, imparting that heat to her body. It's astonishing how fast this can happen. Within minutes she is hot all over and feels herself beginning to sweat. And now there is a painful throbbing in the top of her right foot! Lord, what could that be? She gently slides his hand off her breast and slips out from under his arm. Her foot throbbing stops. She pads silently out the door and into the girls' room, where she gets back into Cammy's bed. Cammy, in her sleep, extends one finger out to touch Susie's arm, and thus they pass the night, mother and daughter.

*Hoagy Carmichael was a beloved Indiana native son and Bud's fifth cousin once removed, who grew up in Bloomington and also graduated from IU and who composed many of his songs in the little cafe where college students hung out, including Bud and Susie, though of course Hoagy was two decades earlier.

Chapter Fourteen

Maggie has convinced Cammy to go with her to Nova Scotia, for the sake of their peace of mind and to avoid feeling guilty for abandoning their mother, even though she abandoned them so long ago. Cammy, somewhat ungraciously, agreed to let Maggie pay for her trip. She felt, as the one who had been gainfully employed her whole life, that she should be able to afford her own travel. But of course she had Matthew to think about. Her oldest child, now forty-five, and just not quite able to make it in the world--and let's be honest, on disability because of mental illness, and still living at home, was a challenge to both her and Dean. He was trying hard to be a "normal" person, but the bipolar thing was pernicious--sometimes it would flare up despite the medication, which Matthew did take faithfully. Consequently he had a hard time keeping a job, although he was brilliant. And the manic phase was way worse than the depressive phase--that's when he would go on wild sprees of buying things he could in no way afford, ridiculous big things, like motorcycles and boats. He was a little like Mr. Toad, from *The Wind in the Willows*. Needless to say, disability did not cover this kind of expense, so they were always having to bail him out of debt.

Cammy didn't talk about this much or complain to Maggie, feeling it was her burden to bear, and also it was a little humiliating, although that's not quite right. It was more that she didn't want to air out all her woes to her sister all the time. But Maggie was certainly aware of it, and sometimes spoke privately of it with Dean. She and Dean were on friendly terms from way back. In fact, Dean had at first been interested in Maggie romantically, when they met at a fraternity party at Memphis State. He was a senior and she a sophomore, and they had a few dates before she decided that he just wasn't her type, but would he mind introducing her to his fraternity brother, that one with the flashy smile, the really good dancer? Dean was crushed, but secretly knew she was right, and so he did introduce them. And Maggie did not hold that against him when that guy turned out to be the cardiologist that done her wrong. She had asked for it, after all. In return for that introduction, she had offered to introduce him to Cammy, who was finishing up her pre-nursing degree--a very practical down-to-earth person, Maggie assured him, unlike herself. He agreed, and the rest, as they say, is history. Dean loved Cammy, and she loved him, even if her younger, more attractive sister had introduced them. Still, it was one of the many tiny twigs of tinder that sometimes ignited a fire of jealousy in Cammy.

One thing that Matthew excelled at was being a grandson. He and Bud were very close, always had been. Being the first of only two grandchildren that Bud had, he was adored from the moment of his birth. Indeed Bud had been the one to bail him out of trouble on several occasions when he went on one of his sprees. It pained Matthew to watch his grandpa grow old and infirm of mind, and he tried to spend as much time with him as he could. That's why Cammy had no qualms about leaving for a week or so, because Matthew was going to stay over there at Bud's to make sure everything was running smoothly. He never went off the rails when he was with Bud. It was a win-win arrangement in Cammy's mind.

Cammy and Dean's other son, David, was not so embraced by Bud, having always been a child he could not really relate to, a boy who preferred watching musicals to going fishing. When David came out as gay, Bud was not quite able to hide his disapproval, having grown up in a time and place where that sort of thing was not talked about in polite circles. He had heard of it, of course, when he was in the army, and there was one guy he had been friends with who may have been that way, but they never discussed it.

David lived in San Francisco now and seldom came home to visit, although he and Matthew were close. Once Cammy and Dean had gone out there to see him, but that hadn't gone well, since at the time he was living in kind of a dive, and was between real jobs and so was "dancing" at a gay bar for some money. Maggie had a soft spot for him and occasionally sent him some money. Susie also did this, unbeknownst to anyone else in the family.

Chapter Fifteen
1957

Susie's second year of teaching is off to a promising start. She is an innovative and creative teacher, able to relate to her students on a person-to-person basis, unlike some teachers. At the end of the school year last spring she had let her class spend two whole days writing scripts and acting out their favorite episodes of "I Love Lucy," which aired its final show on May 6th. Her fellow teachers were somewhat scandalized but that did not faze Susie one bit. Her students adored her and clamored to continue to be in her class the next year, something that the principal vetoed, but several of them did get lucky and end up there.

Right now she is fuming over the news of the day over in Little Rock, the Negro students being denied entrance to the school by the National Guard, as ordered by Governor Faubus. This is outrageous. She has never been overly religious but growing up she did get inculcated with the Catholic concerns about social justice. She decides to do a daring thing in her classroom, an experiment that could get her in trouble, she supposes, but she intends to do it anyway. She is going to declare that all the students with blue eyes in the class will have all the privileges, while those with brown eyes will be denied those and have extra hardships put upon them, not be able to use the water fountains, be at the end of the line always, etc. She is excited to plan this; this has great possibilities, in her mind.

Bud is planning to take the girls with him on a short trip to New York. He has secured spots in the Peanut Gallery for them on the Howdy Doody Show, as a birthday present for Cammy on September 25th. Susie doesn't object to them missing some school. After all, travel is educational, and Maggie is still only six, so what could be the harm? She looks forward to the time alone honestly. It seems she is always tired, even if she does get a full night's sleep, what with teaching, grading papers, fixing meals, doing laundry--laundry! Swear to God, Bud can go through so many clothes. If he wears something for ten minutes, it goes in the dirty clothes hamper. He creates more laundry than her toddlers used to! She can eliminate some of those chores when they are gone--she will just eat frozen chicken pot pies, for one thing. No cooking. Or go out for pizza--a favorite of hers. Bud wants her to come to New York too, but she doesn't want to. One night after the girls are in bed, he dances her around, singing this new song that he heard on the radio—"Susie Q," nuzzling her neck and trying to sweet talk her into it. She laughs and succumbs to his charms in the bedroom, but is firm in her refusal to go to New York. He rolls away and goes to sleep miffed, pulling the covers with him. She gets up and goes to sleep in the girls' room. Again.

When they are gone to New York, she finds she misses them a little bit, but mostly she is reveling in her absolute freedom to do whatever she wants to do, eat what she wants to eat, watch what she wants to watch on TV, sleep soundly all night, and generate hardly any laundry. She gets so much work done! They call from their hotel on Cammy's birthday, after they have been to the Howdy Doody Show and been out to a special fancy birthday dinner. Since it is two hours earlier for Susie, she is just eating her bowl of soup and grilled cheese sandwich (only three dishes to wash!), and she wants to hear all about it in detail. She is thrilled for the girls, and so glad Bud has made this connection with the show. She had made an effort to watch it and see if she could see them in the Peanut Gallery, but the camera just panned quickly at the assembled children and spent the rest of the time on the actors and puppets. Cammy tells her it was the funnest thing she has ever done. They beg to be allowed to go again next year.

"We'll see," says Susie--a tried and true parent response meaning various things, but often meaning No and we'll not mention it again, at least that's what it meant when Susie's mother said it. But today when Susie says it she really means maybe it could happen.

Chapter Sixteen

Despite careful planning, Cammy is still anxious about leaving to go to Nova Scotia. What if something unforeseen happened with Bud? Neither she nor Maggie would be there to take charge of the situation. She didn't want to put that responsibility on Dean (and secretly doubted that he would be fully up to it). Of course she was leaving her phone number and doctors' phone numbers and myriad instructions for every possible contingency that she could imagine to the caregivers, and to Matthew. Oddly, she felt the most confident in Matthew. He knew how to maneuver through all the labyrinthine on-line MyChart health data they had these days, could do that with ease. She continually had to ask him for help in that department. Passwords might be the death of her, is something she frequently said to anyone who might be sympathetic. She had a printed out list of them by her computer (still a desktop PC)--four typewritten pages, double spaced, three columns--and dozens more scribbled hastily in the margin and all over the back side of each paper. User names were scratched out and others penciled in, passwords were scratched out sometimes two or three times ("Forgot your password? Click here"). Her own wireless phone company was one that she was never able to access. Somehow they had different passwords and systems on the phone than on the internet. Oy.

She drives Matthew over to Bud's with his suitcase on her way to Maggie's. She will leave her car there and they will drive to the airport in Maggie's car and park it in a lot until they get back. Somehow Maggie thinks she will be able to deduct this trip as a business expense, or at least she's going to try. Obviously she thinks she's going to have some free time to shop around, grouched Cammy in her mind, realizing at the same time that she herself has no scenarios whatsoever presenting themselves to her when she imagines the trip, the visit. She guessed she expects nothing but drama. But really, what does she know of her mother's life up there? Very little. Perhaps it would just be more like a friendly visit, an exploratory expedition, as it were.

Certainly Susie would be surprised, she envisioned that much. Fine, thought Cammy. She surprised us enough for two lifetimes, let her be surprised for once.

Matthew and Cammy let themselves in the kitchen door. It was mid-afternoon, so no caregivers were there, and Bud was helping himself to a snack--a bar of some kind that Esther had stocked in. It was in fact a nut and seed bar, and Bud was reading the label with snorts of amusement and disgust. "This product contains nuts," he read, incredulously. "Of course it does--it's a goddamn nut bar, for Chrissake." Bud's language had deteriorated a little over the years, but he seemed to be having a particularly lucid moment just then. He continued to grouse about that label all the rest of the afternoon, and Matthew got into it along with him, getting out his laptop and finding social media and internet posts showing ridiculous labels with unnecessary information. They laughed and laughed, and even Cammy joined in until it was time for her to go. She hadn't actually told Bud about the trip, she realized, or why Matthew would be staying there--she figured he could easily be so out of it that she might as well save herself the effort. But he was completely present this day, so then she had to quickly make up a story about where she was going; after all, they were hardly going to tell him that they were going to see Susie--no telling how he would react to that.

"So, Bud, I'll be gone for a few days," she announced with a slight amount of guilt (it might be longer, she knew--they had gotten open-ended tickets, just in case). "Mags and I are going on a little vacation--can you believe it? I don't know when we've ever done anything like that, so we just figured why not?"

Bud looked at his daughter quizzically. "But who will put me to bed?" he asked plaintively.

"That's why Matthew is staying here--he's my stand-in. In fact, he'll be here all the time, not just your bedtime, so that's fun, isn't it?"

"Oh, good, that's fine then. Where are you girls going?"

"Um, we're going to D.C. to visit our cousin!" she lied convincingly.

"Which cousin is that?" he asked, sharp as a tack.

"You know, your cousin Glen's daughter, the one that escaped Indiana."

"Nice, tell her hi from me. She was always my favorite." And with that, he turned back to Matthew and asked if it was time for the news yet.

Cammy blew a kiss to Matthew and went out to her car. Maggie had gotten the cheapest flights she could find, and so they had a seventeen-hour trip ahead of them, involving layovers at Charlotte and Philadelphia, and finally arriving in Halifax tomorrow afternoon. Cammy was not looking forward to it.

Chapter Seventeen

1958

Susie has made herself a little sewing room in one wing of the house, and furnished it with a rocking chair, a table for laying out patterns and cutting, and a sewing machine stand, but also with a cute little daybed she found at an antique store. It has an old quilt on it that her grandmother made, with some pillows that she made herself. The room has good natural light, and everything in there, the walls, the quilt, even the rocking chair, is blue, her favorite color. She likes being in there. She has taken to sleeping in there on the nights she used to go sleep in the girls' room because they squabble over whose bed she ends up in. There has always been the typical sister jealousy between them, and the bed thing is just one more item for them to fight over. Besides, she sleeps better completely alone. Bud is not happy about all the nights she slips away, but he is impotent to change anything. He has learned she is a strong-willed woman when she wants to be. Still, he is becoming a little peevish at her each morning that he awakes to find her gone from their bed. And a peevish morning lends a bad flavor to the rest of the day. Susie is exasperated with him for being peevish. Can the man not understand her predicament? She needs her sleep, for heaven's sake. She has a job teaching and two children and a household to take care of. So, frequently there is testiness between them. An unspoken tension--Bud thinking, will she stay with me tonight? And Susie, not thinking that far ahead but just trying to have things be normal, and check off lists of what she needs to do before bedtime, usually grading papers or folding laundry. If the girls detect tension, they have started retreating to their bedroom, where they play with the Revlon dolls they both got for Christmas. Which is fine with Susie, it's one time they play happily together without fighting.

Bud, in an effort to gain points as a father, and therefore rise in Susie's estimation he hopes, has begun an intensive campaign of taking the girls on outings every Saturday. They have gone to the zoo, down to the riverfront park, and to the Pink Palace, a giant mansion made of pink marble. The property and building were donated to the city as a museum by its builder, the wealthy tycoon Clarence Saunders, founder of the first supermarket chain, Piggly-Wiggly, when he went bankrupt. The girls love going there--you never know what oddities you will see, but the planetarium is their favorite. The museum is developing a wing on the history of Memphis entrepreneurs, a hall of honor for those who have impacted business worldwide. It is Bud's secret ambition to earn a place in that pantheon. Holiday Inn has plans for expanding into Europe, and Bud fully intends to be in on that; if that's not impacting business worldwide, he doesn't know what is.

Susie makes a special effort, on Saturdays when they're gone, to prepare a nice dinner and clean the house.

She pretties herself up to appeal to her husband, and they almost always have a romantic tryst on Saturday nights. She enjoys making love with Bud, but is frequently left feeling that she might be missing something. Since Bud was her one and only partner and sole sexual experience, and having never had any discussion of sex with a grownup when she reached puberty, she is limited to her own private feelings, questions, and conclusions. Confusions is more like it. Sometimes she almost thinks, what is the big deal? Other times she feels something big is about to happen but then it's over and nothing does.

One night she is so close to the mystery when Bud finishes and rolls off of her that she cannot go to sleep. In fact she feels wide awake. She wants more, but more what? She doesn't know what It is, or even if It is. She cuddles with Bud until he falls asleep (two minutes), then gets up and paces around the house. She thinks maybe a late night snack will satisfy her, and goes to the kitchen. She opens cupboards and drawers, looking for something but she doesn't know what. Potato chips? Nope--too fattening. Graham crackers and milk perhaps? Or a banana? Nothing sweet appeals to her. Finally she opens the refrigerator. She went shopping today and so has a nice supply of vegetables in the crisper. Something harmless and calorie-free. Her eye is arrested by a cucumber that is very much the same size and shape as Bud's organ that was so recently inside her. She picks it up--so cool to the touch on a hot night like this. She puts it between her legs under her nightgown, mmm… and then pushes it up a little. Oh my. With a furtive glance around the kitchen, she turns off the light and stretches out on the bench seat of the breakfast nook. Tentatively she experiments with the cucumber. Oh my! After a few seconds she no longer thinks about what she is doing, but just follows the sensations where they lead, and in the process makes a few discoveries. It doesn't take too long before she is fully engrossed in ecstatic exploration. This is amazing! Does everybody know about this? And then suddenly she is engulfed by a giant wave that breaks inside of her and releases the fireworks. And then a series of smaller waves that keep breaking. OH MY! So this is the big deal! How can she have missed out on this all these years? How had nobody told her? Why did Bud not know how to help her to this? Susie is overwhelmed with emotions and questions. She lies peacefully, spent at last, and quite nearly falls asleep right there on the banquette. Jerking herself awake with the thought of Bud's reaction if he found her in the morning, she gets up, turns on the light, examines the cucumber, which doesn't seem to be any the worse for wear, rinses it off, and returns it to the crisper. She pads back to the bedroom and climbs in beside Bud. She sleeps like a rock all night.

Chapter Eighteen

Cammy surprises herself by falling asleep on the plane, something she ordinarily never can do, but Maggie has brought along some kind of cannabis sleep-inducing tincture and convinced her to try a few drops. God knows where she got that in Memphis, but it works. Moreover, her sleep is full of dreams, which it isn't usually. When the plane touches down in Charlotte, where they have a layover but don't have to get off and switch planes, she wakes in a fog of swirling images, sensations, and emotions. Howdy Doody is in Memphis but not Memphis, Cammy is in a prison of some sort, she is drowning but needs to rescue Maggie before she can succumb, Mrs. Wise is holding out a hand to pull her up. Struggling into the light out of that swirling swamp, she cannot move or speak for many minutes. Finally she gets up and makes her way to the tiniest bathroom yet. If they make these any smaller, she thinks, I won't be able to fit in here at all. How do actually obese people do it, she wonders. She splashes cold water on her face and dries it with a paper towel, then looks at herself in the mirror. She's so tired of being old. She has felt old all her life. She sighs, squares her shoulders, and squeezes out the door of the lav. They are about to take off, and she has been instructed to return to her seat and fasten her seat belt.

Ted and Michael are coming to pick them up at the

Halifax airport, per Maggie's arrangement. Cammy's not sure how they will even recognize them, but it turns out to be pretty obvious--two guys standing around with their hands in their pockets at baggage claim scrutinizing every passenger. It doesn't take a great brain to figure it out. Actually it did throw her for a minute that it was two guys and a little girl. Flower had insisted on coming with them. Cammy could never quite believe that Susie had a six-year-old granddaughter and a forty-nine-year-old grandson. It didn't seem possible, so she did the math once again. Ted and Michael had been very young when they lost their mother; she had gotten breast cancer when Ted was four and Michael was only two, and succumbed after a short battle. And then Ted had not married until late in life--he was forty-six, and married a thirty-two-year-old. They had three kids boom boom boom (good Catholics) and then Flower was born, so yep, the math worked out.

Flower rushes over and throws her arms around Maggie. "Oh, you must be Magnolia!" she gushes. "I would recognize that red hair anywhere! Grams has told me all about you!"

"Um, she has?" Maggie glances at Cammy with raised eyebrows.

"And you have got to be Camellia!" Flower pivots to grab Cammy around her waist. "I love that you are named after flowers! I made Mom and Dad change my name legally to Flower after I found out about you. It used to be Estelle. I just love flowers!"

Cammy looks to Ted, who grins sheepishly and

shrugs. Apparently Ted is a man of few words. The men hoist the ladies' bags and they all head out to the garage to the car, Flower chattering non-stop. They have made a plan to stop at Michael's house before proceeding to Susie's, since that's where Cammy and Maggie will be staying. By the time they get there, the sisters from Memphis know everything about Flower's life and are totally charmed by her, and even a bit envious of her relationship with their mother. But Cammy feels relief that, despite Susie's grandparenting experience with her own two sons, which was distant and unfulfilling at best, it appeared that she has a strong connection with at least one child here, in her second life. She is jealous of Ted and Michael suddenly for that.

Michael's home turns out to be a lovely modern Victorian-style lakefront affair in Fall River, the suburb nearest the airport. The guest room has a view of a generous lawn sloping down to the water's edge, where there is a little dock with a speedboat tied up to it. Very nice; the sisters are impressed. They ask Michael if they might have a little rest before going out, they are so very tired from their trip. Of course, of course, he should have thought of that himself. Michael is expansive, gregarious, the complete opposite of Ted. Anything they feel like doing--their wish is his command. And within minutes of "trying out the mattress" on the twin beds, they are fast asleep.

Cammy awakes to Flower softly speaking into her ear. "Aunt Camellia? Is it all right if I call you that? Aunt Meghan sent me to see if you want to get up for dinner."

Cammy slowly opens her eyes; the gloomy light informing her that the day has escaped. She turns her head to Flower, who is holding out a bouquet of fall leaves with one orange dahlia in a glass of water. No one has ever called her "aunt" before, and her heart melts.

"Of course. Of course to both--you may certainly call me Aunt Camellia, and I certainly do want to come to dinner--I'm famished!" she says with a grateful smile. And she rouses herself and her sister and takes Flower's hand, asking, "Will you lead the way for us?" They amble off to a thoroughly amiable dinner with the family they never knew they had, at which they all agree to postpone the visit to Susie's till tomorrow.

Flower has begged to spend the night at Aunt Meghan and Uncle Mike's, so she can be with Cammy and Maggie. When they awake after a glorious night's sleep--cool fresh air coming in the open window!--they find a note slipped under their door. "Gone to early mass, Coffee and croissants in the kitchen to tide you over till we get back for a proper breakfast" signed by Meghan, and another smaller note from Flower, with just a crayoned red heart and one word, "Wellcum." They smile delightedly at each other, put on their robes, and open the door.

Flower is there, having heard them get up, hopping from foot to foot, excitedly awaiting their appearance. "Yay--you're up! I got to skip church today so I could be here when you got up! Do you remember where the kitchen is? Do you want some orange juice with your coffee?"

Maggie looks at Cammy and mouths "Ramona." Cammy smiles and nods. Flower is a lot like the character from the Beverly Cleary books they loved as children, which Susie read to them and at which they all howled with laughter. "The dawnzerly light," Cammy responded with one of their favorite lines, and Maggie's rejoinder, "Sit here for the present." They cackle with glee, which makes Flower smile, though she has no idea what they are laughing about and hopes it isn't her.

Sipping really good coffee in the cozy breakfast area of the spacious kitchen, by a picture window facing the water, buttery croissants melting in her mouth, Cammy feels utterly relaxed. What a life this would be, she thinks. Susie has had it pretty good up here. Why couldn't Susie just move into this house, she wonders. There seems to be plenty of room. She feels worlds of weight lift from her. This trip is turning out to be a dream. Quickly she reminds herself of the daunting task facing them--confrontation and intervention in the affairs of an elder, a parent who is becoming demented but is in denial. This is no vacation. Focus here, woman.

When the churchgoers return, Meghan, a lean, athletic-looking, brisk, no-nonsense type it appears, changes her clothes and gets to work frying bacon and whipping up eggs Benedict for their "real" breakfast. Michael, or Mike as they all call him here (except Ted, who calls him Mick), lounges with the sisters in the bay window area and chatters happily about peripheral subjects, avoiding any mention of Susie. He is a real estate agent, hence very skilled at schmoozing and small talk. They find him eminently likable. They have two sons in high school, nice boys, very involved in hockey of course--they each play on different teams, so Mike and Meghan are stretched between those games like a macramé dreamcatcher.

At the big table, over a delicious brunch really, Maggie thinks, rather than breakfast, Meghan brings up the possibility of having a day of touring around the area, putting off the Susie thing yet again. "I mean, this is your chance to see a whole new place that you've never seen and will most likely never visit again. It seems a shame to waste it. We could go out to Cape Breton--it's such a gorgeous fall day, the foliage will be breathtaking!"

The sisters trade looks. They can read each other's minds much of the time. Right now both of their minds are thinking, well she's right really, it does seem a shame to come all this way and not enjoy it just a little bit. One more day isn't going to change anything. It's not like Susie is expecting us--she won't know the difference if we come today or tomorrow. Cammy shrugs, and the decision is made wordlessly. They allow themselves to be beguiled into a day of tourism and even to let go of guilt and immerse themselves in it. The day is spent in glorious exploration of the North Atlantic seacoast, complete with a lobster dinner that puts Pappy and Jimmy's Lobster Shack in Memphis to shame.

Chapter Nineteen

1959

The New Year is rung in with all due excitement in the Benson household. Everything is just going swimmingly. The girls are doing great in school (Cammy in sixth grade, Maggie in third), both avid readers and good spellers. That is important to Susie; she is a stickler on spelling and proper usage. As a teacher, Susie has a reputation for being demanding but also fun. Bud is moving ever upward in the Holiday Inn corporation, traveling often to open up new motels all over the country. He is bringing home lots of money. Susie is very proud of him, and proud to be his wife. He is so handsome, even more so now that he has that early streak of white hair that runs in his family (his mother was completely white by the age of twenty-five). He turns heads everywhere they go. They are a fairly glamorous couple, and she revels in it.

Susie hardly ever sleeps in her sewing room anymore. Now that she knows what she wants out of sex, she can kind of encourage things that further that. She has one good friend at school, another teacher, and sometimes they get together and have "girl talks." Cammy and Maggie are now both in Bluebirds, the junior Camp Fire Girl organization, and on the days they have their meetings, Susie stays late at school so she can pick them up on her way home. On those days, she and Connie go into the teacher's lounge and put on a pot of coffee, smoke, and chat about life in general, but somehow it always comes around to intimate talk eventually. This came about when Susie first encountered Connie in the lounge one day, visibly upset and trying to calm herself. Susie immediately gave her a hug and asked what was wrong. What was wrong was that the principal, one Joseph Choplick, had come on to Connie in a very aggressive way when she was in his office discussing a child. Practically an assault, Connie said. Which Susie, though shocked, could actually believe, because Choplick was a greasy little man who always seemed to be leering at teachers as if picturing them naked. Connie is Italian, and from New Jersey, so she knew how to quickly put the kibosh on that, but still. Her husband Rick is in the Navy, stationed at Millington, the naval base in north Memphis, and Joe Choplick would be no match for him if it came to that. Connie is vastly more informed and experienced than Susie and, since their relationship has developed into that of friends who share intimate secrets, has given Susie a number of tips and techniques she might try with Bud to get him to be more considerate of her needs, guiding his fingers to certain areas, and so forth. Even once, putting her mouth to Susie's ear, even though no one else was in the room, she whispered something so shocking that Susie's eyes almost popped out of her head. Susie has tried some of these to some effect, though Bud has expressed his objection to "being used like a machine," as he thinks of it. So, she makes sure to always have a nice cucumber on hand just in case.

One night, she finds she needs to get up and retrieve that cucumber to do its job before she can get back into her bed and have a satisfied sleep all night. She is in her sewing room, on the daybed, having an erotic encounter with a vegetable, when she hears the toilet flush in the hall bathroom. Uh-oh, Bud must have gotten up for some reason--he always just falls dead asleep after sex, something must be wrong. She holds her breath, waiting, frozen in place, *in flagrante* with herself, as it were.

Bud has indeed gotten up to use the bathroom. Something he ate must not have agreed with him. He notices the empty space in his bed where Susie should be, and then sees the faint light coming from her sewing room. Huh, he thinks. She doesn't really sleep in there anymore. He pads down the hallway toward the room to see what's going on. Susie can hear his footfalls in the silent house, but she is paralyzed. A very lapsed Catholic, she nonetheless sends up a fervent prayer to whatever saint is the patron saint of secrecy--after all, there must be one, there is one for literally everything else in the world--but still she is unable to move. What is wrong with her? Why does she not at least close her legs and turn over as if sleeping? But no, it's almost as if some little part of her wants to be caught out.

He peeks into the room. "Suze?" The look of consternation that comes over his face is almost comical. "What are you doing??"

That is the precise moment it all falls apart; that tableau is fixed forever in Susie's memory--the dim lamp light in the blue room intensifying the colors, the feel of the quilt beneath her legs. She cannot say anything, has suddenly become not only paralyzed but struck mute too. What could she possibly say? It's blatantly obvious what she's doing. Bud's face is a kaleidoscope of emotion--shock, then dismay, hurt, and finally rage. Most of all his male ego is badly bruised.

"What's going on here? Look at you! Didn't we just...??? You're fucking yourself with a cucumber??" Susie recoils from just his using that word, which he never does. At the same time, her insides are aflame with nearly fulfilled desire, and somehow hearing him say that releases some kind of permission to get raw, and it overtakes her. She continues pleasuring herself as he watches, taunting, daring him to do something. What has come over her???

"You disgusting slut! What are you--a nymphomaniac or something?" He wants to take out his member and shake it in her face and say, "This isn't good enough for you??" Wants to throw her up against the wall and fuck her violently, asking, "Is this what you want? Huh?" But he is not that kind of man, so he curbs himself. Through clenched teeth he says, "Well, if you like Mr. Green better than me, then that's the way it will be. Have fun with him." And he turns on his heel, storms back into the bedroom, and slams the door.

The next morning is awkward. Neither of them has slept at all. Bud tossed and turned all night, and Susie cried a lot and finally fell into a deep dream state at dawn. By the time she gets up, he has gone out, and the girls are having cereal in front of the TV watching Saturday morning cartoons. She is not hungry at all, but puts on a show of eating for the girls' sake. She sits down with them on the couch and watches cartoons. This is strange behavior for her, but the girls don't seem to notice. Susie sits there with dull eyes, staring at the TV set without really seeing. She cannot believe what she has done. She has just detonated a hand grenade in the middle of her perfect life. There is no way to undo what has been done, she knows this in her bones. She thinks of all the things she could have done instead of what she did--she could have made light of it, or tried explaining it to him calmly, or even tried to get him involved, but she did none of those.

Deep down she knows Bud is firmly of the mind that a woman should be able to magically climax at the same time as her husband during vaginal penetration, period. This will indeed prove to be a fatal blow to their marriage. The next year and a half will be hell, as gradually all the heretofore invisible fault lines will begin to rumble and shift, that otherwise would have remained benign and still.

Chapter Twenty

SCORPIO SEASON GUIDE

VISIT A GRAVEYARD
ATTEND TO A SACRED MYSTERY
BE WILLING TO SEE SOMETHING YOU'VE KEPT HIDDEN FROM YOURSELF
RECONNECT WITH THE EROTIC
COMMIT YOURSELF TO RADICAL INTIMACY WITH THE WORLD
IDENTIFY WHERE YOUR GREATEST POWER COMES FROM
SPEND TIME IN THE PLACE IN YOUR LIFE THAT REQUIRES THE MOST HEALING
HONOR THE DEAD
RESEARCH YOUR ANCESTORS
TRUST YOUR POWERS OF REGENERATION

†

In the early hours of Monday morning Maggie opened her laptop to see her daily horoscope, something she had gotten in the habit of doing several years ago when she had a psychic reading to help guide her through yet another failed relationship. No one was up yet. Maggie had woken up and been unable to get back to sleep (something that plagued her fairly often), and so she had just gotten up and was sitting in Meghan and Mike's comfortable family room, musing and amusing herself. She cast an eye around the room for the bookshelf, just because she couldn't help it, saw nothing of interest there. No classics at all, but it seemed they were fans of prolific Canadian authors--they had the complete Margaret Atwood (so far), all of Louise Penny, and so forth. All hardbacks, as though they were a book club edition or something, totally worthless in value as collectibles. Maggie was not much of a reader, per se. She was interested in books more for their market value than for their literary qualities. Still, she did recognize those authors as very good reading.

She mused about their very nice day yesterday as tourists. They had ended up not going all the way to Cape Breton but stayed closer to home, doing some city stuff in Halifax, and then taking a tour of Fisherman's Cove, a 200-year-old working fishing village, all cuted up of course for tourism, but fun nonetheless. Cammy had gotten fairly worn out with all the walking, but Maggie actually enjoyed it immensely. She wondered what had drawn Susie here in the first place, but was not surprised that she stayed. She was getting the idea that Susie had led a wonderful life here.

She returned her attention to the Scorpio season guide, the horoscope that she favored over any other. "Be willing to see something you've kept hidden from yourself." Okay, here she was, seeing Susie's environs that had been hidden from her. Surely that counted. "Spend time in the place in your life that requires the most healing." Again, here she was, in Susie's life, about to face her mother, the person with whom she needed the most healing. She guessed she was on the right path. "Research your ancestors." Truly, she was trying. After all, her mother was her nearest ancestor. And, by huge coincidence, she could also check off "Visit a graveyard," since at Flower's insistence yesterday, they had stopped by the cemetery where Grampa Don (Susie's husband) was buried, so she could show Cammy and Maggie, though why she thought they would want to see it was a mystery. It wasn't far out of the way, so Mike had indulged her once again. Maggie suspected Mike of feeling partial to Flower because all he had were two sons who, as far as Maggie could tell, were not interested in anything at all besides hockey, and had zero personality. She knew that could not possibly be right, but after one day that was her opinion. And indeed, the cemetery was utterly charming, picturesque and peaceful. They placed a handful of colorful leaves on his grave, which was next to his first wife's plot, and Maggie found herself silently thanking Don for being a good husband to Susie. "Honor the dead." Check.

Maggie's reverie was interrupted by the advent of the morning--the boys having to get up and get ready for school, Meghan making their breakfast, Mike getting a call. Cammy came padding out in her robe and sat down with Maggie in the family room, yawning and stretching. "Oh, I slept so great! I feel ready for anything now."

As if on cue, Mike came in, his phone cupped to his ear. "Okay, yep, we'll be there as soon as we can. Everyone's just getting up. Okay, see ya." He looked at the sisters. "That was Ted. He got a call from the Life Alert thing that we gave Mom." The Life Alert thing was something else Cammy and Maggie had not known about. "I guess she fell or something, and couldn't get up, and of course she wasn't wearing the thing around her neck like she's supposed to but she was able to drag herself over to where it was on a night stand by the bed."

"Is she okay??" asked the sisters simultaneously.

"Yeah, they took her to the emergency room, but everything checked out. They don't know why she fell, and she doesn't remember anything. That was in the middle of the night. They're releasing her to go home now--Ted is there. I told him we'd meet him at the house. You have time to eat some breakfast first."

There was nothing to say. They got up and went to dress themselves. Just as they sat down to a cup of coffee, Cammy's phone rang. It was Matthew. Here we go, she thought. It all falls apart at the same time.

Chapter Twenty-one

1959

Life went on, as it does, despite that hand grenade that had exploded into their lives. For the sake of the girls, and appearances, and just the putting of one foot in front of another, an uneasy truce settled over the household. Bud started going to bed quite early, saying he was tired and had a busy day ahead, and closing the door to the bedroom, which Susie took to mean she was not welcome in his bed. Fine. She slept in her sewing room. They spoke in terse, utilitarian sentences, strictly about the logistics of their life.

One day Susie had a late faculty meeting after school, and called Bud to ask if he would fix dinner. Of course he would, came the answer. When she got home, just in time to sit down with the family to eat, he served up BLT's and soup for himself and the girls, but on her plate was simply a large cucumber. Her face flamed red and she pressed her lips together. The girls were looking at her worriedly.

"You know what?" she managed to rasp out. "Our meeting went so long that someone sent out for pizza, so I'm not really hungry anyway. I will eat this though, so that I'll have a vegetable," and she picked up the cucumber and, looking straight at Bud, stuck the whole end of it in her mouth, and walked out of the room. After that, cucumbers started showing up everywhere. Bud must have clipped pictures of them out of the grocery ads, out of domestic arts magazines, anywhere he could. Susie would find them next to her toothbrush, or in her coffee cup, by her makeup mirror. It wore on her over time, and one day at school Connie looked at her, at the dark circles under her eyes, and pulled her into the teacher's lounge during one recess.

"Honey, you look awful. What's going on?" And that brought the whole thing tumbling out. Susie was relieved just to have someone to confess to, as it seemed to her she was doing, to get it off her chest. "Okay, you and me are going to take a little field trip. No more cucumbers for you--you deserve the real thing."

Susie was alarmed at the sound of that. What on earth was she talking about? The real thing? So, on the day of the Bluebird meeting, where the girls would be occupied until nearly dinnertime, Connie put Susie in her car and drove her to a seamy area of downtown that Susie had never been in. She felt very uncomfortable there, but Connie seemed to know what she was doing; in they went to a small dark store that sold pornography and sex toys, as they were referred to in the store. Susie had never even imagined such a place in her wildest fantasies. She was so embarrassed to be there she could hardly look around. With Connie's guidance and advice, whispered in as few words as possible, she handed over her cash in exchange for a vibrator, which she hid in her purse even though it was in a plain brown paper bag.

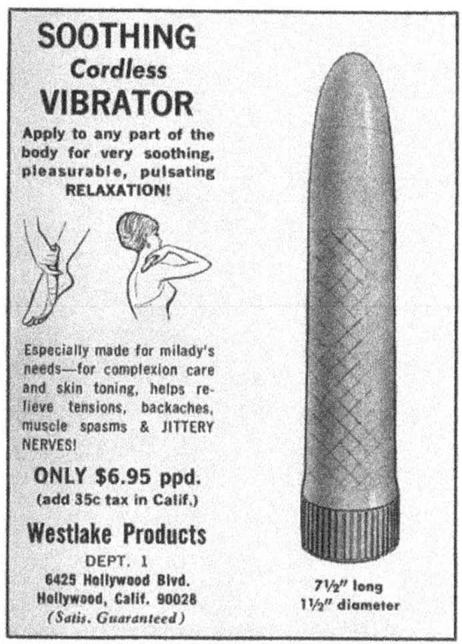

When they were safely back in the car, Susie fumbled for words. "Um, is it... do you think... I mean, do lots of people..."

"Do lots of people use things like this?" Connie completed Susie's question for her, laughing. "Of course. These things go back all the way to prehistory. Archeologists have found sex toys in every culture they have studied. Don't worry—you're not the first woman to want a different kind of stimulation. I have one myself."

"Does Rick know about this?"

"Sure--we sometimes use it together. What's wrong with that?"

Susie was amazed and then relieved, and then ashamed at her ignorance, and finally, more angry at Bud for his ignorance and resistance to her needs. I mean, if Connie's husband could be all right with this, why couldn't Bud?

She couldn't wait to get home and hide it in her sewing room. She exhorted Connie to drive faster as they hurried back to school, where Susie jumped into her own car and drove to the Bluebird leader's house. She tried to imagine the Bluebird leader, one Margaret Boyd, a prim-and-proper Memphis lady, using the vibrator, and nearly broke out laughing.

Cammy and Maggie were happy that Mama seemed in such a good mood for once. It was of course not true, as Bud and Susie pretended, that the girls did not notice what was going on. It was true that they spent more and more time in their room playing together, but not necessarily happily. Cammy became hypervigilant for signs of tension in the household, and, as children will do, assumed responsibility for it. She took it upon herself to try to keep Maggie from doing anything that might upset the parents. And, it must be said, at times took advantage of the situation to be mean to Maggie and then bully her into not tattling for fear of upsetting them.

The Saturday outings with Bud had ceased to happen, just when Cammy was hoping they could go out and cruise by Graceland. She kept up with the Elvis Presley gossip--what with the scandalous stepmother takeover after Gladys died last year, resulting in one day Elvis summoning a moving van and banishing Vernon and his new wife Dee and all their possessions, it was all pretty dishy stuff. But these days Bud was always out golfing on the weekends. He had decided they should join a country club, so that he could golf and the girls could swim and have tennis lessons and so forth. Mama hated golf and didn't care who knew it, so she never went with him or did anything there at all, unless they all went out to dinner there, which had happened a few times but not lately. Susie didn't care much for the folks there that Bud was wanting to cozy up to--she felt nothing in common with them, especially when they talked about their Negro help. The feeling was reciprocal too—the other women did not work outside the home (or even much inside the home), and so were unable to relate to Susie's teaching career. Their sugary veneer was transparent to Susie and frankly disgusted her.

Perhaps the fresh air and exercise did Bud good, or perhaps he noticed that there never seemed to be cucumbers in the house anymore, real ones that is. Susie had become good at using her new friend BOB--Connie's name for her vibrator, standing for Battery-operated Boyfriend, which Susie loved and appropriated. And one day she had said in front of everyone that she "didn't like cucumbers anymore," looking pointedly at Bud. At any rate, one Saturday night, after weeks and weeks of a closed bedroom door, Susie noticed that it was open. She wondered if that was deliberate or not, and decided to see what would happen if she just got into bed as if everything was normal again. Also she missed her bed--the daybed in the sewing room did not have a good firm mattress, and her back was starting to hurt. Bud was asleep when she slid into the bed beside him. She tried not to disturb or touch him, but since he had gotten used to sleeping alone, he had expanded into the whole space. Rolling over, he flung his arm out and it landed on her soft breast. They both gasped, and what ensued was desperate sex, fast and a little rough, as if he thought that's what she might like, or just because. Susie was left wanting more, as usual, than he had given, so after she was sure he was asleep, she crept out of bed and down the hall to her sewing room and BOB. So much faster and easier than a cucumber! BOB got straight to the point, and she was back in bed in short order, sleeping comfortably.

The next morning Bud woke up pleased with himself and the world in general, gazed fondly at Susie still asleep, got up, and wrote his to-do list for the day while he drank coffee he had brewed. Then he fixed a nice breakfast for the family--their favorite Sunday morning Daddy breakfast, crazy sandwiches he called them--open-faced grilled cheese with tomatoes and bacon on top, and Worcestershire sauce drizzled over it all. Everyone experienced, though they could not have put words to it, a sort of ambient relaxing, a long exhale, as it were. Suddenly not every little thing was infused with possible catastrophic significance. Life went on after all.

Chapter Twenty-two

By the time the crew from Michael's got to Susie's house, she was fast asleep. Ted had insisted she lie down, after being up all night in the emergency room and all, and within minutes she was out. So Ted, Michael, Cammy, Maggie, Meghan, and Ted's wife Anne, fortified with pastries that Anne had picked up on the way there, all sat down in the living room and had The Talk. What to do about Susie. The doctor had said she must not live alone anymore. Caregivers were horribly expensive--the money would run out after a while, and then what? Likewise eldercare homes. Meghan and Anne were subtly adamant that she would not be living in either of their homes; they did not intend to be her nursemaids. These were all discussed at length. The pastries and two pots of coffee were consumed. And what about the Jamaicans? All assembled quietly looked at each other, waiting for a miracle idea.

A small noise made them turn toward the door to the hallway. There stood Susie, looking so frail, a halo of white hair framing her haggard, confused face. Her gaze rested on each of the Canadians until she recognized them, and then it landed on Cammy and Maggie. Her watery eyes widened, and an overjoyed look of relief came over her. "Take me home," was all she said, but in those quavering three words were a lifetime of emotion, exhaustion, desperation, and longing. She was clutching a bandanna in both hands and burying her face in it. It was Bud's bandanna from the war, when each bomber pilot got a special bandanna printed with maps of where they were, so they could find their way back to Allied territory if they were shot down and escaped.

Maggie reached out for Cammy's hand. She turned her face to Cammy, questioning, pleading. "Mama," she said, her voice breaking. Cammy closed her eyes and took a deep breath, and gave a slight nod of her head. And so it was decided. They would take her home, to Memphis.

"Commit yourself to radical intimacy with the world."
"Trust your powers of regeneration."

Maggie knew this was the right thing. It felt right, way down deep inside her. Sometimes, you just have to go with those gut feelings. Now only three guidances were left.

"Reconnect with the erotic."
"Identify where your greatest power comes from."
"Attend to a sacred mystery."

Chapter Twenty-three

Once it was decided, then the Canadians swung into gear to make it happen as quickly as it could. By happy coincidence, Michael was in real estate, and so could help out with all of that part of it. The major work was the dismantling of the home that Susie and Don had built and lived in all these years. For the remainder of Monday, Cammy and Maggie decided to just be there with their mom and see how she was doing, talk to her, and determine if she could understand what they thought she wanted to do, if they were all on the same page, or if it was too late for any cognizant participation from Susie.

They helped her get dressed and then they all had a bite to eat--Meghan went into Susie's kitchen and whipped up a minor feast out of miscellany that she found in Susie's refrigerator. Really it was like that radio show where you call in to stump the chef with the ingredients you have on hand, thought Cammy, who listened regularly to that show on NPR. Meghan was a wonder.

They decided to proceed as though Susie were completely present, brain-wise, and so after lunch the girls asked her to show them around the place, since they hadn't really been there before. Well, Maggie had, but Cammy didn't know that, and anyway it had been years. The Canadians left them there for the afternoon, while they went back to their various obligations on a Monday.

The girls were curious about all the lovely hooked rugs everywhere--on the floor as rugs, on the walls as tapestries, on the couch as pillows, in the kitchen as pot holders. "Mama--where did you get all these hooked rug things? And where is your sewing machine? I don't see any evidence of a sewing room," Cammy asked casually. Susie had always referred to her "sewing group," and since she was a sewer, that made sense; Cammy had assumed that since there was a sewing room in the house she left, she would have one in her next house.

Susie had indeed been somewhat revived mentally by some food and by the appearance of her daughters. "Oh, I've never had a sewing room up here," she said. Then she got a faraway look in her eyes for a few minutes. They all pictured the blue room in Memphis. It was still there, exactly as she had left it, like everything else in the house. The girls politely waited to see if the memory would pass. It did. "You really don't need a sewing room to make these--they don't require any special equipment other than one simple little tool that you can make from a nail and a dowel. And a simple wooden frame, and burlap. That's all."

"Mama! Are you saying you made these rugs?? They're beautiful!" Maggie was nonplussed. Items of this quality would fetch a fortune at craft shows. Not that she would sell any of them--they were too precious.

"Sure I did! How I got started on it was one weekend after the boys were gone, Don and I drove out to Cape Breton for a weekend jaunt. We went all the way up to Cheticamp, at the northern tip of the Cape. Rug hooking is huge all over the Maritime Provinces--it's what they did in the winter when there was no fishing. It got them through the Great Depression. Very interesting. So, we went into a shop there and I was hooked. Ha! I just made a pun! Pretty good for an old demented lady, eh?"

Cammy and Maggie were stunned and delighted that their mother was so... so... entertaining and talented. "So, you don't sew then?"

"No, not really. Sew the odd button back on a sweater once in a while."

"But... but you were always talking about your sewing group," Cammy said plaintively.

"Oh, it was just easier to say that than explain the whole hooking thing, and that group," Susie responded with a vague wave of her hand.

"What group? The hookers have a group?" Maggie asked, and then they all burst out laughing. Little by little they coaxed out of her the details that she dismissed as nothing of importance, the fact that there were craft shops all over the place up here where she sold her work.

Ever since she had retired from teaching, this had been her main hobby. She had even started designing patterns and selling them at those shops. She was a popular artist. The sisters were aghast that they had never known one thing about this; they felt left out once again.

Chapter Twenty-four

Matthew is a fairly light sleeper, and he wakes up when he hears noise coming from Bud's bedroom. He goes to investigate. His mom is a worrier, so he has been instructed ad nauseum to not slack on paying attention to Bud at all times. Personally he thinks the old man is pretty okay most of the time. As he nears the room though, he can hear what the sounds are--they are getting louder. Bud is crying, sobbing; he is distraught. In front of him is a whole drawer of his dresser upside down on the floor, its contents strewn about. Pictures of Susie. All the same. Her school portrait from the fall of 1960, just before she left them. Dozens of them, three different sizes, but mostly the wallet size. None of them in mint condition.

"Susie!! Why did you leave me???" he roars, tearing at his hair. He is approaching hysteria now. Matthew becomes alarmed. They never discussed what to do if Bud got like this, indeed he doesn't know if Bud has ever been like this. Cammy left Esther's number in case Matthew got in over his head with a situation. But it is four in the morning--he doesn't feel he could or should call her now. Which is why he calls Cammy in Nova Scotia early that Monday morning. He stands in the hallway, practically whispering into the phone, so that Cammy has to continually say "What?" and he has to repeat what he says. He thinks he should stay near Bud and keep an eye on him, but he doesn't want him to overhear the call. It doesn't matter though, because Bud is nowhere near this time and place. Matthew holds the phone toward the room, and Cammy can even hear him storming and bellowing.

"What should I do Mom? I called you because I didn't want to wake Esther up at four a.m. I don't know what to do."

Cammy closes her eyes and waits for the calm that precedes the knowing. Then it comes. "Go in there, Matthew. Go to him, and put your arms around him and hold him. Say soothing things but don't be dismissive. Recognize his pain. Acknowledge his distress. Got it? Can you do that?"

Matthew nods, as if she could see that. It's more for himself, that nod. He walks in, puts the phone down on the bed, still on, and puts his arms around Bud. Bud looks at him in confusion. "Who are you? Get away from me!"

"It's me, Grampa. Matthew. I see you're missing Gramma tonight. I'm sorry you're sad." Bud slumps in Matthew's arms, and they practically fall onto the bed together, barely missing the cell phone. Bud dissolves into great heaving sobs, and holds onto Matthew as if he were drowning. Cammy can hear all this, and it goes on and on until eventually the sobs subside and end. She can hear Matthew lay him down in the bed and pull the covers up to his ears the way he likes them, murmuring softly to him as he does all this. She is so proud of Matthew at that moment she could burst.

Matthew grabs the phone off the bed and tiptoes out

of the room, leaving a nightlight on. This must be what it's like to have kids, he thinks. He goes back to his room but still speaks in hushed tones. "I did it Mom. I did just what you said, and it worked! You are a genius."

"No, just experienced. I am a nurse after all, remember? And a parent. But you did it, Matthew! You have demonstrated great patience and understanding with your grandfather and I thank you for it. He is lucky to have you there. I am lucky to have you there--thank you."

And so she is able to have her breakfast and go to face her mother with peace restored to her.

Chapter Twenty-five

When Ted comes back late that afternoon to pick up Cammy and Maggie, he is in a foul mood. The bank has alerted him that Susie had, on Saturday, gone to the supermarket and successfully wired money to the Jamaicans that way. Four thousand this time. They decide to start the process of moving tomorrow. Cammy and Maggie opt to spend the night there with Susie, just in case, and to further cement their relationship for taking her back to Memphis. Ted shows them the guest rooms--his and Michael's old bedrooms, which still contain remnants of their pre-adult lives. Susie and Don didn't have a lot of guests apparently, and just never erased the traces of the boys.

Ted calls Michael to apprise him of the situation, and Michael takes charge. "Okay, we're all going out to dinner together. My treat. Least I can do, under the circumstances. And then tomorrow we'll hit it hard. Sound like a plan?" Everyone agrees that it does.

He will bring the sisters' suitcases over so they will be able to change clothes, freshen up, and so forth.

Cammy goes into the bathroom and calls Matthew. She wants an update on Bud. He answers right away, as if he expected her call. "Hi hon--how is he today after that horrific night episode?"

"He's really disoriented today, Mom. I've not been

able to interact with him normally at all. Also--I forgot to tell you about the drawerful of pictures of Gramma."

"Drawerful of pictures?"

"Yeah--he had pulled out a whole drawer that was full of school portrait pictures of Gramma; it must have been maybe just before she left you all, when she was still teaching at Colonial. They were strewn all over the floor. That's what he was screaming at."

"I didn't know he had a drawerful of her pictures. Which drawer was it? I've never seen that drawer."

"It's the small one in his big dresser--it doesn't matter, Mom. Anyway, I got in there before he woke up and cleaned them up and put them back. Didn't want to set him off again."

"Okay, well good for you, hon. That was good thinking." Cammy was distracted by the idea of a drawerful of Susie pictures. "Just stay close today and tell Viola and Esther about what happened, and let them handle him for now, 'kay? And keep me posted."

"I will, Mom. Bye. Love you."

At dinner that evening, it seems to all that Susie understands what the plan is that they are making and it is what she wants. They agree that her task in the morning will be to go through her bookshelves and choose what books she absolutely wants to keep, and then decide what to do with the others. Then winnow her way through the art, memorabilia, and finally, the hooked rugs. The temporary plan is for Maggie to install Susie in her house, since it is large and she lives alone. That just makes sense. The money really is an issue, due to Susie's

Jamaican extortions. So they will have to investigate elder home situations in Memphis when they get there. But in any case she cannot take all her worldly possessions--she has to shed things now. Susie nods and doesn't look confused. Furniture--what about the furniture? They all look around. It's hard hammering out all the details. Are they going to put things in storage? (for when? Susie is old.) Are they going to send a trunk of belongings? A pallet, by freight? Are they going to rent a truck and drive back to Memphis with big things? Maggie's house already has a full contingent of furnishings.

Meghan steps forward with an ambitious plan--she will organize a cadre of hockey moms, and they will throw together a jumble sale as a benefit for the teams. If they work feverishly, they can have it the following weekend, what with social media advertising and digital communication. Is Susie ready for that? Of course the family will get to pick things they want to keep before the public has at it. Susie nods vaguely. She looks tired. Michael calls for the check and they pile into his car and return to her house for the night.

Susie dreams. She is in Sister Mary Francis's office getting her knuckles rapped.

"Susannah York--you are a disgrace to this school, to your family and the church. You never finish anything. You seem to have an aversion to finishing tasks you are given. Why is this? *Thwack!* Your mother tells me you are the same at home--doing some of what you are asked but never all of it. Putting your clean laundry away, for instance. Your teacher tells me you do most of a math page but not all of it. Likewise your catechism teacher. *Thwack!* Young lady, you will not advance until you learn to finish what you've begun. Do you understand? *Thwack!* Susie nods, tears running down her cheeks, but she is not a child anymore. She has suddenly morphed into her full grownup self, and she is in front of the whole congregation at the church she attends here, and the priest is the one chastising her. "You have sinned against your sacred vow of marriage. You must go back and salvage what is left of it. This is your penance. Do you understand?" *Thwack!*

Maggie wakes early the next morning. She has been sleeping in Ted's old room, and Cammy in Michael's old room. Twin beds, one to a room. She takes the opportunity before all the hullabaloo starts to look around. There is a small bookshelf there, despite Susie having told Maggie more than once that the boys didn't read. A few classics--*Call of the Wild, Moby Dick,* some high school and college yearbooks, and one peculiar gem that she almost didn't see--*A Wrinkle in Time,* complete with original dust jacket! What!? She grabs it off the shelf and gingerly opens the front cover. There is an inscription:

To Ted - you might not be quite old enough to appreciate this yet, but it is a treasure awaiting you. Susie, 1964

1964. The year Susie and Don unveiled their relationship. Two years after the book was first published. This is a valuable book, Maggie knows that, but she's not sure how much it could bring. She digs her laptop out of her suitcase only to discover that it has run out of battery. Looking around for a place to plug it in, she hears sounds coming from Susie's room. She steps out into the hall and listens, and hearing what sounds like weeping, moves swiftly to the room. Knocking softly on the door, she does not wait but opens it.

"Mama--oh Mama!" Susie is wandering around the room in a daze, moaning and whimpering. "Mama--what's wrong? Are you sad because you agreed to move back to Memphis? Do you want to change your mind?"

Susie looks at her warily, as if not sure of who she is, but at the mention of Memphis perks up. "Memphis. Yes, back to Memphis. I must go back to Memphis." Her tone of voice is that of someone in a hypnotic trance. "Can you take me there?" She really doesn't know who Maggie is or what is going on. "I must get back to my class--they will be acting up since I've been gone so long."

Chapter Twenty-six

1959

Life resumes normality for the Bensons. Bud suspects nothing amiss in his relationship with Susie, but then Bud is a man not overly partial to introspection. He prefers action. Early in the spring, he has decided to move ahead with his plan to build a bomb shelter in the backyard. Now that Castro has succeeded in his coup and become dictator of Cuba and allied himself with Russia, Bud doesn't know what might happen. The cold war could turn hot. And the inclusion of Hawaii and Alaska, making us a country of fifty states, did nothing to reassure Bud. Alaska isn't that far from Russia. He has called a construction company and arranged for them to come in late March and dig out the shelter.

Thus, one day when Susie arrives home from school with the girls in tow, they find a giant hole in their yard, with piles of lumber and equipment lying around, including a concrete mixer. Bud has somehow neglected to inform Susie of his decision--not to mention consult with her about it and get her input. She is completely outraged. She storms around in a fit of pique, pacing the perimeter of the yard. Bud has gone back to work after overseeing the beginning of the project, so he is not there, and the workers are done for the day and gone. So she doesn't really even know for sure what the thing is for, but she has a pretty good suspicion, because of previous ideas Bud has floated about doing this. Suddenly she is seized with an idea. She stops pacing, clasps her hands together, and considers. Yes, this might work. A little smile plays around her mouth.

Cammy watches her mother carefully, although things have not been so tense around the house lately. And because once hypervigilant, always prone to hypervigilance, she intuits that things are about to get tense again. When Susie goes in the house, Cammy tells Maggie to come in too, and they settle in front of the TV, because Susie is in there. She is on the phone with Connie, speaking in low tones. When she sees the girls come in, she ends the conversation but makes another call. This one is to the secretary of the school. "Helen--this is Susie. I'm afraid you'll have to find a sub for me tomorrow--all of a sudden I feel a little cold coming on. Yes, I'll let you know about any other days tomorrow. Thanks." Cammy looks at her quizzically, but Maggie is oblivious, immersed in the TV show. Susie returns Cammy's look defiantly and says, "I can take a day off if I want--I have plenty of sick days I can use."

That night Susie does not even mention the hole in the ground to Bud, though he is looking at her expectantly, awaiting her reaction. She does not give him the satisfaction of an argument. She doesn't care about the cold war heating up. Well, she does, but thinks surely another nuclear bomb would never be dropped. Hadn't we all been sufficiently horrified by Hiroshima to know better than that? She does not intend to let it ruin her backyard.

The next morning she trundles the girls off to school without her. They can walk the distance--it's only a mile and a half. Bud leaves earlier than they do, so he doesn't notice that she is not getting ready for work, though when he says goodbye he does so with a slightly questioning demeanor. Waiting for her to react to the hole. She says nothing, gives him a big kiss on the lips, and sends him off.

When the construction crew shows up, she is waiting for them with new instructions. She assures them that she and her husband have reconsidered and now have a different plan, and it won't be that much of a deviation from the original design. When Bud gets home that evening, he is satisfied with the progress they have made--the concrete walls and floor are poured and drying. Still Susie says nothing about it. Two more days go by, and Bud inspects the work each evening. Now the roof beams are in place. He guesses Susie has just accepted the fact of it and is living with it. He would be wrong--he should know her better than that. The girls are curious about it and he tells them as much as he thinks they need to know about the reason for it, which is vague and non-threatening. He doesn't want to scare them. He doesn't realize that they have duck-and-cover drills at school, and that they know the reason why. When they ask Susie about it, she just smiles a mysterious smile and says, "We'll see."

The next day when Bud gets home, he is in for a shock. The roof is in place, but it is entirely glass panels! And there are concrete raised beds poured along each of the two longer sides of the rectangle, filled with soil, and shelving along the back wall, and a potting table with a sink. There is a short slanted path down to the door from yard level. Bud is apoplectic.

Susie strolls out to meet him in the yard, two gin and tonics in her hands. "Hello darling," she smiles, handing him one of the drinks. "Do you like my modification of your little war room? I think it's much more conducive to positive energy." This whole design was something she had seen in the latest issue of *Look* magazine in the teacher's lounge at school, which she had read thoroughly while eating her lunch. So many interesting articles! Except for the Notre Dame Football one; she did not read that. It stirred up old and unpleasant memories of her father's relentless cheerleading for Notre Dame.

<u>LOOK</u> March 3, 1959

"The Case For The American Woman" by Diane Trilling; "A Catholic In 1960," Betsy Palmer; Havana Cuba Memo; Notre Dame Football; Peter Townsend; Springhill, Nova Scotia.

It was on a page facing the "Catholic In 1960" article that there was a short feature all about "positive energy." With suggested ways to achieve it, one of which was to get close to the earth through gardening, and showed a picture of someone in a greenhouse converted from an old root cellar.

Bud is so angry he is actually speechless. He feels like throwing the drink, dashing it against the concrete, but he is not that kind of man, so he doesn't. Instead, he chugs it down, glares daggers at Susie, and stalks away. Dinner that night is a frigid affair. The girls are very worried. A major fault line has just shifted.

Susie spends the rest of the spring ordering seeds, planting seeds, and generally puttering around in her greenhouse. She finds she loves it in there--the temperature is always perfect, warmth supplied by the sun above and the earth below, and she truly does feel positive energy when she digs in the dirt.

Chapter Twenty-seven

In fairly short order, out of a sense of urgency for the jumble sale, or really an estate sale is what Maggie considered it, two piles of stuff emerged--one for the sale and the other for discarding. The sisters went about dismantling Susie's rooms, with her in tow, asking her in loud voices, as if she were hard of hearing, which she was not, whether she wanted to keep something or not. She followed them around obediently and gave vague answers. They were not sure she understood what was happening. Ted and the others came along and pitched in, and Meghan started cleaning. Ted glanced around his old room and said he wanted nothing in there. Maggie debated with herself whether to tell him about the book--the agreement was that anything not claimed was up for grabs. She gnawed on this ethical dilemma all day as she went about sorting other stuff, but in the end had to give in and do the right thing. After her laptop was recharged, she took a small break from the work, sat down with a cup of coffee, and looked up what *A Wrinkle in Time* with original dust jacket could bring. It was quite a bit--perhaps $11,000. Maggie approached Ted with the book in hand. "Hey Ted--I found this in your old room."

He looked at it for a second, opened it and read Susie's inscription. A rueful and apologetic look made his rather bland face look suddenly filled with character. "Ah, I remember when she gave me this. She had such high hopes that I would be someone she could share great books with, someone who read. Sadly, I was not. I'm afraid I was a big disappointment to her in that way. I never even read this."

"Well, it's uh... it may be valuable. It's a collectible book now."

"What do you mean?" Ted had no idea that books could accumulate monetary value just by being old.

"I mean that with the right buyer, this book could bring in thousands of dollars."

"Oh, piddle on that. I can't bother with that kind of nonsense. I don't have time. Do you want it?"

Maggie's heart leaped. "Well, if you're sure you don't. I mean, I kind of do that for a living."

"Really? Perfect. You take it and get what you can for it--after all, you spent a lot of money getting up here and everything." Maggie was euphoric the rest of the day.

The stuff that did not get sorted into either pile, sale or discard, was the stuff hardest to decide about, of course. In the end, it was evident that there was going to be more than they had really wanted to ship to Memphis. Susie had not wanted to let go of a few special pieces of furniture--a rocking chair that Don's grandfather had built out of ash wood, a small table with a secret drawer hidden in it, and also she decided to take her rug hooking frame and supplies, in case she felt like continuing with that hobby. It became slowly apparent to both sisters, though neither one admitted it, that they needed to rent a small van and drive home to Memphis with Susie and her possessions. Perhaps they could squeak by with an SUV, if they packed it right.

Chapter Twenty-eight

Summer 1959

Now, ever since the Greenhouse Incident, it was Susie's turn to try to earn points with Bud by being a Good Mother. She took the girls to the country club pool for swimming lessons every day for weeks on end, and sometimes afterwards they would all lounge around on the deck eating cheeseburgers and French fries with Cokes, wait for it to digest a little, and then swim and play in the pool for the rest of the afternoon. She accompanied Bud and the girls to see his beloved Memphis Chicks (short for Chickasaw, not chickens) baseball team play at Russwood Park, which smelled like popcorn and beer, and turned her stomach a bit, but she ignored that and cheered mightily for the boys. She made a special effort to look nice and ask him about his work and be really interested each evening when he returned home. She even suggested going to the club for dinner more than once, despite her disdain for the other wives. Bud was happy to do that, as he did like to show her off. Since spending all that time at the pool, she had turned a dark tan, and with a strapless sundress on, she looked very good indeed. In the bedroom Bud succumbed to her charms again and again.

In early August, though, Susie had to go to Indiana. Her father had died. She thought it only proper that the girls go too, although Bud felt he could not take the time off from work. So he stayed home and they went to the funeral of their emotionally distant grandfather who had hardly taken any notice of their existence.

The first Sunday afternoon while they were gone, Bud went to Russwood Park to see the Chicks play, and for some goldurned reason they were playing a Cuban team--the Havana Kings. Two of Castro's henchmen, Camilo Cienfuegos and another, were actually there in their revolutionary uniforms, and Chicks manager Luke Appling actually shook their hands! Bud was appalled, furious, fuming, and practically snarling the more he thought about it as he drove home. What were they up to? Cuba wasn't that far away from Florida. Were they scoping out Memphis as part of their plan to take over the western hemisphere? He stormed around the house, drinking several shots of whiskey as he got more and more worked up over it.

Recognizing that he was really too upset, he went outside to calm down a bit. A plan, he needed to have a plan of some kind, any kind, just to make himself feel better. His eye fell upon the greenhouse, now having done its work for the season, sitting empty, sunk in the middle of the yard. Aha! It was just that simple--he would call the construction crew in the morning and arrange for them to come back and undo the greenhouse and make the bomb shelter after all. Susie had had her little joke, done her little gardening thing, and now it was over. It was his turn. Who knew what would happen with Cuba and the Russians? The Russians had nuclear weapons now--the world was not safe.

He called Susie at her mother's house in Indianapolis, ostensibly to commiserate with her on the loss of her father and see how she was doing, but really to buy some time for his project. He asked her to take a few extra days and go down to his hometown so the girls could visit their grandma on his side. She agreed, since it was summer vacation and they had nothing else pressing to do. She had always liked that little town anyway, and she liked Bud's mother.

Thus it was that when Susie and the girls did finally get home from Indiana in mid-August, they saw, for the second time, a bomb shelter in their backyard. Except this time it was completely finished. Including the atomic symbol on the front of the foot- thick metal door. And the words "Fallout Shelter" below that, as if there was any doubt.

Chapter Twenty-nine

The estate sale has happened, very successfully, thanks largely to Meghan and the hockey moms. Almost everything sold to the public, and what didn't sell, the supportive sport-loving families bought. The rest of the family spent time together but not at the sale. Everyone advises against watching one's beloved possessions being sold off. Susie stayed at Michael's, with Cammy and Maggie, and they played games and ordered in food (Meghan being occupied with the sale), and even the boys joined in, after a prod from Michael regarding how this might be their last and best time with their granny.

Somehow Susie seems to have forgotten all about the Jamaicans, and Michael has surreptitiously blocked them from her phone. So that's solved. Although one day while they were cleaning Susie's house, a local policeman came to the door checking to see if Susie was alright, because someone named Tony who claimed to be her nephew could not get ahold of her. It was only then that Susie's brain allowed a glimmer of her former frontal lobe function to float back to her. Her wide eyes met those of her two girls in an agreement of revelation. One broken bond is repaired.

The girls are careful to be near Susie physically almost all the time, fearing another fall. Cammy is well aware, as a nurse, that falls in the elderly are often the cause of the beginning of the end--worse dementia and pneumonia being two of the most common. They keep a hand near her elbow, or around her back. She seems to appreciate it, and with good food and family around, she appears nearly normal much of the time.

A van has been rented and is in the process of being packed with the things Susie wants to keep. They drive that van around to all the shops where Susie has her work for sale, and arrangements are made as to how to reroute the reimbursement for those items that sell. There were quite a few to visit, and once again the sisters are struck by their mother's local fame, at least in the craft arena.

Michael is going to list the house as soon as the final appraisal is done. He has high expectations that it might sell, but also it might need a few improvements made. It is, after all, a house of a certain age. At least painting and new carpet.

The night before they are to leave, Ted and Anne and their brood, including a sad but still excited Flower, come over to Michael's for a goodbye party. Meghan has made Susie's favorite foods, including poutine. Anne has put together a photo album of all their best family moments, and one of the teenagers made a framed collage of warm wishes and declarations of love for her. It's very moving and filled with tears and laughter. Susie seems overwhelmed by it. Flower refuses to leave her side, and promises to write to her a lot. Flower writes down Maggie's address and gives it to Anne, who smiles and puts it in her pocket, pats her daughter, and agrees that they will.

Thanks to everyone from everyone for everything goes all around the room. Lots of hugging ensues, and then, finally, it is over.

Cammy and Maggie help Susie to bed, and then themselves to a nightcap of well-aged Scotch in Michael's den. They have planned out what route they will take down through the states and they are actually kind of excited about a road trip through New England in the fall. They've never done that kind of thing before. Never breached the gap from sisters to friends, really.

They sit with drinks in hand, staring out into the dark night, lights twinkling across the water, not saying anything for a while. Then Cammy reaches her hand out to find Maggie's hand.

"Remember that one birthday party you had, where we had a campfire and roasted marshmallows?" she asked.

"You mean the time when you made marshmallows for all my friends and put bouillon cubes inside them? That time?"

"Yes, that time. I'd like to apologize for that."

Maggie paused a beat, then chuckled softly. "Well, at least that was one birthday party no one will ever forget going to." She squeezes Cammy's hand.

Chapter Thirty

Fall 1959

Susie is so dispirited by Bud's installation of the bomb shelter that she loses her spunk to fight it. It's too late. There is nothing to be done. She stops going into the backyard at all. Abandons all her gardening efforts; the flowerbeds go to weeds. Bud still mows the grass of course, but otherwise it is barren. She doesn't even sit out on the porch anymore--the shelter is visible from the swing that hangs there.

Anyway, by the time they get back from Indiana, it's time for her to put her classroom together for the school year, which will start the week before Labor Day. She is looking forward to this year because Maggie will be in the classroom right next to hers. She likes the idea of that so she can know exactly how Maggie does in school, and also maybe keep her from getting in trouble, as she has done once or twice in the first two grades. If Maggie thinks her mother could pop her head in the door anytime, that might curb that little redheaded rascal a bit. She is thinking about setting up a daily behavior report from Maggie's teacher too, something she recently learned in a workshop.

Bud, now that it is his turn to be on the defensive over the fallout shelter, decides to take the girls to New York again for Cammy's birthday, and to the Howdy Doody

Show, where he has maintained his close ties. The girls had clamored to go back after that first time, but it hadn't happened that he had any work-related missions in the vicinity. This year Holiday Inn is opening a new facility in New York, just outside the city, so it will work out fine. They can stay there and just go in to the studio for the show. He asks Susie, of course, to go with them, but is not surprised by her polite refusal.

Bud has been lobbying for Susie to have another baby, something she has no interest in. She makes love with him his way, makes her visits to the sewing room and BOB when necessary, sleeps in his bed, and they can all get along. She sees no reason to rock the boat. Nor does she want to put her career on pause again. She loves her job. Also, two children is just right, in her mind. They continue to use the diaphragm mostly, but once in a while they use a condom.

About two weeks before the trip to New York, Bud gets amorous, and says he will use a condom. He goes into the bathroom to put it on, which Susie finds odd. Especially since when he comes back, he is still holding it in his hand. He says with an embarrassed smile, "I forgot I don't like to put this on until the last minute." Huh, she thinks.

The next day is Saturday, the working woman's day to catch up on cleaning and household chores. As Susie empties the bathroom waste basket, where Bud's used condom resides, she notices something. For some reason, the tissues all around it are all stuck together more than usual. She looks at it more closely. The semen has leaked out. She picks it up. There is a small puncture in the very tip of the rubber. Oh no. She cannot believe that he would do this to her. She tried to think when her last period had been. Her very hazy idea of some kind of "rhythm method" she had heard about in Catholic school allowed her to think that perhaps the timing had been good in terms of the sperm missing the egg. Also, that hole was really tiny--surely not that many could get through. She decided to hold off on jumping ahead of herself. Maybe nothing would come of it.

It's while they are gone to New York that Susie starts having the signs--nausea, tiredness, and sore breasts. This can't be happening, she thinks. She tries to do some things to perhaps mitigate all that, like hot baths, and deep breathing, which she has read about in the *Sunset* magazine in the teacher's lounge, but really, isn't it just common sense? Her discomfort just continues and gets worse.

Bud and the girls will not be home for a few more days; Bud takes advantage of those trips to see the city, the classic New York landmarks--the Empire State Building, the Statue of Liberty, the Museum of Natural History. He and Susie are in complete agreement that travel is vital to an education as much as school is. And with his salary, they can afford it. Of course their lodging is free, at the Inns. So she doesn't care how long they stay. Particularly this time--she does not want her roiling emotions showing and Bud asking her what's wrong. She does, however, plan to confront him with the evidence of his crime. To that end she has saved the offending item, wrapped in a washcloth in the bathroom.

In spite of the girls being in New York and thus missing their Bluebird meeting, Susie and Connie have their regular coffee, smoke, and chat session after school. Once again Connie notices how she looks.

"Are you pregnant by any chance?" Connie doesn't mess around. Susie admires Connie's decisiveness, yet she is a little surprised by the accuracy of her guess.

"How can you tell?" she wants to know.

"I dunno--it's just, you look tired but then there's this kind of glow too."

Susie grabs Connie's hand. "Connie--I don't want a baby." And, in the whispering voice they use for intimate sharing, even though they are the only ones there, she tells her about the punctured condom. Connie's brows draw together and her eyes squint, that universal expression that means "uh-uh."

"Ooh--that snake! He cannot get away with that. We have to do something to get revenge. Men just can't keep women home barefoot and pregnant anymore! Times are changing." Little did the women know that as they spoke, the first steps toward the birth control pill were happening. But it wasn't in time for them "Well, do you want to do something about it? I can help you."

"What are you talking about?"

"Do you want to, you know, end the pregnancy?"

Susie is shocked. "I can't do that! It's illegal, and besides, I'm Catholic! And how exactly could you help me do that???"

"Women do it all the time, honey. It happens. I can

find out. I know people."

"Out of the question. Do not even think of that. It will work out. The baby will be due right at the end of the school year, then I'll take the summer off and..."

"And then Bud will let you come back to work in September? You're dreaming, Suze. And you know it."

"Maybe not. You said it yourself--times are changing. I have a really good babysitter--maybe she would be a nanny. Yes! That's it--Mrs. Wise will be the nanny. I'll make Bud agree to it!"

Chapter Thirty-one

Driving through New England in the fall was indeed a breathtaking experience. You just didn't want to look away or close your eyes, thought Cammy when it was her turn to be in the passenger seat. They made sure to pull off into quaint little villages for their meals and pit stops, and to get out and stretch their legs. Susie seemed appreciative of these forays, admiring any crafts they saw for sale, and eating pretty heartily for an old lady, although occasionally she asked, "Where are we going?" in a very interested way, as if they were on a family vacation. Which in a way they were. Maggie briefly entertained the thought of trying to shop some of the hooked rugs in the van to the craft galleries they saw, but discarded that idea as being too unwieldy to keep track of.

They continued south through Massachusetts to New York. As they were skirting the city, it was getting to be time to think about stopping for the night. Looming ahead of them next to the Turnpike was the old familiar Holiday Inn sign, with the big yellow arrow. Susie was gazing out the window when she spotted it. "Oh--let's stay there for the night!" she exclaimed, with uncharacteristic clarity.

The sisters looked at each other with consternation. "Really, Mama?" asked Cammy. "The Holiday Inn?"

"Holiday Inns, I'll have you know, are very good places to stay. They're clean, and very handy to get to, and they're all the same. You know what you're getting."

Reluctantly, Maggie pulled off on the exit and turned in the direction of the Inn. They tried to distract Susie by calling attention to all the other advertisements for lodging--"Look, there's one with a heated swimming pool!" Or, "This one has a free breakfast buffet!" But Susie was adamantly focused for once.

"I have very fond memories of Holiday Inns. I'd like to be in one again, please."

Maggie and Cammy sat in grim silence; this was the very Holiday Inn they had stayed at with Bud when they came to New York for Cammy's birthdays and to see the Howdy Doody Show. It had held happy memories for them until that last time, 1960. That was the point at which the tenuous thread that held their family together had broken for good. New York was ruined for them, and then home was ruined.

Nevertheless, they checked in and were given the keys to Room 117, two queen beds. They had decided wordlessly that it would be best to stay together with Susie. They could sleep together, or one with Susie, depending. They freshened up and went down to see what kind of dinner options there were. Holiday Inns had never incorporated restaurants into their facilities, but just decided to be the magnet around which restaurants would flock. Bud was on the team that made that decision. It worked out.

This one had lots of Asian choices--Japanese, Korean, Russian, Chinese, but they selected one called Sea Food Boil, a plain-sounding name that perfectly described what it offered. Maggie and Susie ordered the King crab legs, and Cammy ordered a lobster roll. It was very good, and familiar to Susie. As they were wiping their buttery fingers with the warm wet rag that came with the meal, Cammy's phone buzzed. It was Matthew. She thought she had better answer it, as she hadn't talked to him for several days. "Hi Matt--how's it going?"

Susie was at that moment not disoriented. She was aware of what was going on, though still prone to doing unpredictable things, and when she heard Cammy say "Hi Matt" she perked up, and grabbed the phone out of Cammy's hand. "Matthew! Hi! It's your grandmother! Guess what? I'm coming back! I'll be there with you pretty soon! Won't that be fun?"

Matthew was a little surprised, but recovered quickly. He had not actually been informed about the decision as to what to do with Susie, Cammy realized in that moment.

Not that he had any voice in the matter. It wouldn't affect him at all, is what she thought, falling so easily into that trap of dualism that everything is separate and not connected to every other thing. "Grandma! Take it easy on an old guy like me--don't spring shocking surprises on us!" he teased. Susie laughed delightedly.

"Okay, no more, I promise. How old are you anyway? I've lost track."

"I'm forty-five," he replied seriously.

Susie looked thoughtful at this news. "And not married?" she asked. "By the time I was your age, I had already left one life and embarked on another. You've yet to embark on one."

Matthew smiled wryly to himself on his end. "I guess I'm a late bloomer, Grandma. Where are you gonna live when you get here?"

Susie looked a little confused at that point, but she was aware enough to know where they planned to take her; it was to live with Maggie, wasn't it? "Oh, well, you have to ask your mother about that, I guess," she said, resorting to old-age vagueness for convenience.

"Okay. Can you give the phone back to her then? Thanks. Bye Grandma--see you soon." Cammy took the phone back and got up from the table and walked away a little.

"Hi. I guess I got so busy packing and everything that I just forgot to tell you about our decision. Everything happened so fast. She's coming to live with Aunt Maggie. How are things there?"

"He's been worse ever since that time I called in the

middle of the night. But manageable. But then he had another episode yesterday. With the drawerful of pictures. Esther was here to see it though, and actually she handled it completely. And masterfully, I might add."

"Tell me," Cammy demanded, still mystified by the whole drawerful of pictures she hadn't seen.

"We heard him crying. In his room. I was in my room, and I thought he was napping. Esther was making dinner, but then we both heard him crying really loud. We hurried in there, and there he was with the pictures all in his lap and all over the floor. There must be a hundred of them. I like to never got 'em all picked up when the whole thing was over." Cammy waited, impatient to hear the whole story, not the details. "Anyway, Esther knew about the pictures, I realized then, because she didn't act surprised to see them. She did the strangest thing then. She went in the living room to the old stereo player he has, and put on a record—"Memphis in June" by that Hoagy Carmichael. Turned it up so he could hear it in the bedroom, then came back in and sat down beside him on the bed and put her hand on his shoulder. And then she picked up one of the pictures and said, 'Remember where I found this one, Mistah B?' And he said, 'Where?', and she said, 'Taped inside the lid of the flour canister in the pantry.' And they both laughed. She did that for several other ones too--they had all been found in really obscure places. Esther must have noticed me looking totally confused, because then she said, 'Your grandmama left these pictures hidden all over the house, and every time anybody found one, this one here saved it. He likes to look at them ever' so often, don't you, Mistah B?' Bud nodded his head sadly. He seemed completely lucid. And then she went on and asked him about Grandma, what she had looked like, what it was he loved most about her, all kinds of really specific stuff like that. And he knew all the answers! She was the best listener too! And when the record ended, he was just totally recovered from the outburst, and he followed her out to the kitchen. Later she explained to me that music helps banish the dementia for the time it's on--it's the latest in scientific breakthroughs on dementia treatments apparently. Somehow synapses in the brain get cleared of their fog or something. I don't understand it, but it works!"

"Wow," said Cammy. "That's amazing. I haven't heard of that. I'm so grateful for Esther--she's such a good caregiver."

"She really is," agreed Matthew. "So, where are you and when will you be back?"

"We are just outside of New York, probably be back in three days, maybe two. I'm glad to know that trick, Matt. Thanks for calling and telling me. It might come in handy for me here. With Susie, it's in and out of confusion--you just never know where you are."

"I'm getting a good education in it myself," he said. "Okay, see you soon. Love you."

Chapter Thirty-two
Christmas 1959

Although Memphis is often a warm-wintered place, once in a while it snows or there is an ice storm. 1959, though, was not one of those years (cloudy, high of 56), except in Bud and Susie's bedroom. Ever since he and the girls returned from their trip to New York, Susie has refused to sleep with him, in the carnal sense. She sleeps in the same bed, but that's it. When she wagged the punctured condom in front of him his first night back, he was flustered and obviously guilty. She reproached him for it relentlessly, accusing him of ignoring her wishes entirely and treating her like a child, instead of an equal partner in the marriage. Plus, she has gone to the doctor and sure enough, she is pregnant, three months along by Christmas. Complete with morning sickness and various aches and pains. The temperature in their relationship has settled in at frigid on her part, and guilty but aggrieved on his part.

The girls go on pretending not to notice anything, though they communicate between themselves with certain looks. They have one look that means "uh oh--let's go outside, something is about to turn ugly." Another look means "maybe this would be a safe time to ask for..." whatever it is they want at the moment. They of course notice that Susie is more tired than usual, and try to help out around the house, or at least they comply when asked to do their chores. Both Mama and Daddy seem distracted much of the time, so the girls are expert at waiting for attention. When they finally have it, they take advantage of it to get all their needs met. They have let "Santa" know what they want for Christmas, though of course they know that Santa is the grownups who love you. But this is a storyline everyone goes along with in the Benson household. They have written Santa letters asking for Barbie dolls--the biggest new toy of the year, as they still enjoy playing dolls together. And they leave little hints around the house, like ads for Barbie in the Sunday Commercial Appeal, reminiscent of Bud's cucumber clipping period, which they of course noticed too, at least Cammy did, though she didn't know the reason for it.

Since there is no extended family anywhere near the Bensons, they always just fix the big traditional dinner all by and for themselves: turkey, two kinds of dressing (Pepperidge Farm for stuffing, and southern cornbread dressing as a side dish), rolls, mashed potatoes and gravy, cranberry sauce, yams, green bean casserole, pecan pie and pumpkin pie. It's a lot of work. This year Susie tells Bud she just cannot face it. They will have to do something else. She wouldn't mind going to Britling's--a cafeteria that she really likes. Bud is quietly appalled at this idea--the idea of eating Christmas dinner at a cafeteria!--but is at a loss as to alternatives. He certainly can't do it all by himself. Perhaps the girls could pitch in. Yes, that's it--they can do things to earn their Camp Fire beads in kitchencraft. He will propose that to them immediately. They can work on shopping lists, recipes, table planning, all of it. Surely there's an orange bead in there somewhere for this exact thing.

Bud does enlist the girls in this endeavor, and all are enthused about it, though he mixes in some regret and concern for Susie's condition, with the accompanying implication that the daughters need to do it as their familial duty. But it's okay--Mama can coach them from the sidelines. A tree has also been procured, and Bud and the girls do all the decorating, with Susie lying on the couch, trying to appear interested, but really just wanting to sleep. At least the Christmas vacation has started, so she doesn't have to go to work. She doesn't understand this pregnancy--it seems harder than her other two somehow. She is so tired all the time. Or, she wonders, does she secretly resent it so much that she imagines all the tiredness? Will she even love this new baby? Fears and doubts flit through her semi-conscious mind.

The day before Christmas, Cammy and Maggie carefully follow Susie's instructions for putting together the cornbread dressing. They have to chop onions and celery and sauté them in butter, with some sage, salt, and pepper. Then add that to the cornbread (made yesterday and crumbled up in a bowl), with eggs and chicken broth, pour it into a casserole dish and bake for an hour at 350. This is an old tradition in Susie's family, passed down orally--no written recipe--from her father's mother and her mother before her. Southern women, acquired by the Scotch-Irish ancestors who came west to the frontier of Indiana via North Carolina, Kentucky, and Tennessee. It is Susie's favorite food, just about. The girls are very proud of themselves for making it just right, with Mama's approval. They store it overnight in the Frigidaire, to be heated the next day.

Christmas Day dawns grey and dreary, not warm, but not too cold. Just blah. Bud gets up really early and puts the turkey in the oven, makes coffee, and warms up cinnamon rolls he picked up from the bakery. He puts on Christmas music, and then waits for the girls to come racing out of their room and begin tearing into the gifts, of which there are many. By a supreme effort, Susie has managed to sew an outfit for each girl--matching dresses in a nice red and purple plaid with a white Peter Pan collar. She drags herself out of bed and into the living room, where Bud hands her a cup of coffee. The pile of gifts is so large that opening them all takes up most of the morning. At last they are finished, and have time to play with the toys, the most exciting of which are the Barbie dolls. Susie, however, is about to make them write their thank-you notes to Grandma Fon (Florence's nickname) for the matching sets of pajamas. ("No Mama--please not now!" rejoined by "Better to get it out of the way than put it off and it never gets done.") She stands up to get the stationery out of the desk, and gasps with pain, grabbing her abdomen. Then, to everyone's horror, a wet bloody mess falls out of her onto the floor. She screams, then faints, as the girls wail in terror, and Bud is paralyzed with disbelief.

Then it is all just a blur: ambulance for Mama, frantic drive with Daddy to the hospital, emergency room at Baptist Hospital downtown, and the eeriness of Christmas everywhere rendering even the hospital seemingly empty, only a few people on duty today. Loneliness is the ambient temperature there, and it seeps in through all your senses. Finally Mama is given a room for overnight--she will be fine, but they want to keep an eye on her for a day. She has lost a lot of blood--she will need to rest and recover from this for a while. Daddy really wants to go to the room and stay with her, but children are not allowed in hospitals, other than the emergency room, so how can he do that? He could take them home and call Mrs. Wise and see if he could wrench her away from whatever Christmas thing she had going on, then go back to the hospital. But it is Christmas. What about the girls? What about their dinner? Suddenly he remembers the turkey in the oven. Oh my God--that makes the decision. They have to go home immediately before the thing burns up. He grabs each girl by the hand and they race back through the echoing hallways and out to the parking lot, and Bud drives at top speed along the dark empty streets. Presumably everyone is having a nice Christmas dinner somewhere, or at least that is Bud's self-pitying internal attitude, though of course that is not true.

Bursting into the house, Bud is relieved to smell only a very hot smell, but no smoke. He yanks the oven open and pulls out the bird, which by now has been cooked twice as long as it should have. They all look at each other. What to do? Bud clears his throat. "Let's have a glance at it and just see what kind of shape it's in, okay?" The girls are close to tears, but they nod. He bravely takes it out of the roasting pan, sets it on a platter, and takes the knife to it. He picks out a piece with his fingers and examines it, gives it to Cammy for tasting. "Maybe it's not so bad," he says.

Cammy puts it in her mouth and tries to chew, but it's too hard. Basically it has become jerky. She looks at Bud, still trying to chew, and shakes her head in bitter disappointment. All of a sudden they are all aware of being starving--there haven't been any actual meals that day, just random snacks--tangerines, nuts, and candy canes. There had been candy canes in the emergency waiting room.

Bud closes his eyes and massages his forehead. Nothing else was even started for the dinner: the dressing sat cold in the refrigerator, the potatoes still comfortably in their skins on the counter, cans of green beans and mushroom soup unopened. "Okay girls--you know what we're gonna do?" He was putting on such a good show for them. "Britling's. We're going to Britling's for Christmas dinner. That's what Mama wanted in the first place. And then you can tell her all about it. She'll be glad."

And they did. They were the last people there, in a big room with many tables, all empty. Cold bright lights, shiny floor. Loneliness was definitely the temperature there.

Chapter Thirty-three

"Music has been utilized
in interventions
related to pain, stroke, anxiety,
Parkinson's, dementia,
and depression, to mention a few."
– Marko Ahtisaari

After the seafood dinner, the sisters took Susie back up to their room in the Inn. She was wound up and excited after talking to Matthew, elated and proud that she knew who he was. She didn't seem sleepy at all, so they turned on the TV and all sat up in the beds watching various screens--Maggie (at Cammy's behest) was looking up music and dementia on her laptop, Cammy was texting Dean to see how he was doing at home by himself. Susie was shouting out suggestions at Wheel of Fortune for solving the puzzle and sometimes they made sense. Maggie, having discovered lots of fascinating neuro-science facts about music and dementia, switched over to her phone and started texting Cammy, so they were having a private, silent conversation about their mother right in front of her. Maggie was all for trying this stuff out right then and there. Find some of Susie's favorite music--a personal playlist, as it were--and play it on the phone. Maggie thought that if they ever wanted to get some answers to all their questions over the years, it could be now.

"Like what?" questioned Cammy.

"Like, everything," Maggie replied, somewhat annoyed. "Like, why did you leave? What was going on? Did Daddy cheat on you? And what was that on Christmas Day??" In fact, no one ever had taken the trouble to sit the girls down and tell them frankly that Susie had miscarried the baby. They actually were not even sure that she was pregnant--all they knew for sure was that she was really, really tired. Beyond that, their imaginations supplied terrible, frightening possibilities. The wet bloody mess that had dropped out of her that day was not really recognizable as anything. For all they knew, Mama's insides were rotten and falling out. Was it the dreaded cancer, a term that they had heard but that was so terrifying in its shroud of mystery that they couldn't begin to comprehend what it was. The whole Christmas season would be forevermore overshadowed in their subconscious with a feeling of dread and depression, something Maggie had actually had to thrash out for herself with therapy. Not Cammy though, to her it was plainly and painfully obvious. That and September 25th, her birthday, later that next year. Maybe now was when she could tell Mama about that, if she was lucid.

Cammy agreed that they could make a playlist, and then maybe just see what happened when they played it for her. They went back and forth about what should be on it, finally deciding on several songs they remember their parents liking, including such diverse styles as Johnny Cash and Nat King Cole, Patsy Cline and Doris Day ("Que Sera Sera"). This took a while. Wheel of Fortune bled into Jeopardy! with no lessening interest on Susie's part, who loved to show off her knowledge. After they had a list of about ten songs, Cammy returned to her phone to play Candy Crush while Maggie found the songs and selected them to a playlist. When it was ready, she texted Cammy, who nodded and switched off her phone. They each took a deep breath and looked at Susie. She was fast asleep.

Chapter Thirty-four
1960

A pall fell over the Benson household that New Year's Day. With Susie just home from the hospital but still very weak, there was of course no New Year's Eve partying at all. Normal activity decrescendoed to a fraction of its former vitality. Mama did not return to work right away, Daddy seemed to be taking more time off to take care of basic chores around the house. It was a wound that kept oozing pus, and the girls felt it palpably. Each of them of course pretended--this was the way of their family, their era perhaps, or perhaps every era--that everything was all right. Or at least they adjusted and went along, because what else was there to do? Cammy and Maggie were bundled off to school when it resumed, Mama stayed home. When they came home each afternoon, Mama would ask about their day, what they were studying, and what was going on at school in general, but they could tell she wasn't ready to go back. She asked the right questions, and was not really listening to their answers, but gazing off into the middle distance, listlessly.

Then they came home with this news: Maggie had a friend in Susie's classroom, right next to hers. They had been playing together on the playground at recess, and the friend, Clara, was complaining about the substitute teacher that was filling in for Susie.

"She's mean," Clara whined. "She doesn't let us have any fun--just work work work! And spelling bees! I hate spelling bees! And she can't teach math--we haven't gotten any papers back this whole time, so we don't really know how we're doing. You should see the huge pile of papers to grade!"

Maggie reported all this to Mama, who instantly sat up at attention. "What? She's not grading the papers?" Susie was fastidious about keeping up with the grading. "I have to call Connie right away." She reached for the phone and dialed Connie's home number. Together they hatched a plan for Connie to collect all the ungraded papers, then Susie would send Bud with a briefcase to pick them up after school the next day. That was Camp Fire day for the girls.

Bud showed up with the briefcase the next afternoon. Connie had been missing Susie a lot, and worried sick about her health. Here was her chance to ask Bud all about everything, what had really happened, and how

Susie was doing. She invited him into the teacher's lounge and made a pot of coffee, the way she and Susie used to on Camp Fire days. They sat at a table and smoked and talked. Bud told her everything--from the shocking and horrible miscarriage in the late morning to the cold and lonely Christmas dinner at Britling's that evening. It was good for him to have someone to confide in--he hadn't let anyone at work in on what had actually happened, and Connie was totally sympathetic. He confessed that he thought Susie was depressed more than anything, and that's why she wasn't up and about. Connie didn't let on that she knew about the punctured condom, and that perhaps there was a tiny element of anger and blame going on too. What she did was suggest that he surprise her with something unexpected to rouse her from her lethargy.

"Like what?" he asked. Bud was all ideas when it came to work, but not so much in the relationship realm.

"Mm... maybe something personal. Intimate even. In the bedroom, if you know what I mean."

Bud looked confused. "Uh, I'm not sure I do. Could you be more specific?"

"I mean, try doing something you've never done before in that department. Like... kissing her. All over." She looked at Bud as she emphasized the last two words. "Any ideas yet?"

Bud blushed furiously, gathered up the papers, and stuffed them in the briefcase. "I have to go pick up the girls now. Thanks for all your help." And he made a hasty exit. Connie rolled her eyes. For such a handsome man and a man of the world, in a way, he was still somewhat of a backwoods hick. She would take her own Navy seaman over him any day, even though his ears did stick straight out.

Nevertheless, Bud thought about what she said.

When Susie saw the briefcase full of math papers, she immediately went into action and started grading. She sat at her desk with her red pencil and her copy of the teacher's textbook, and didn't look up for two hours. But at dinner, she seemed energized, not tired.

"Clearly, they have not been properly taught how to do long division. Their attempts at it are pathetic. I am going to have to go back and do it all over again, or they'll be behind the rest of the grade in math," she announced in a firm voice. Bud and Cammy and Maggie exchanged surreptitious glances of hope. Maggie said, "Oh Mama--your class will be so happy--they miss you so much!" And that was that.

Chapter Thirty-five

It felt like the last leg of their journey, hurtling west on I-40 toward Tennessee. It was a beautiful fall day and the ladies were in good spirits, having found a Cracker Barrel restaurant for lunch. Susie was in heaven because she got to eat some fried okra--one of her favorite Southern foods. It wasn't the best she'd ever had, but beggars can't be choosers, she reasoned.

Maggie casually took out her phone and hooked it up to the Bluetooth in the car and put on the playlist they had generated the other night. It did seem as though Susie's brain brightened up then. She started humming along with the music, even singing the words after a few minutes. Maggie and Cammy were each waiting for the other to make a move.

Suddenly Cammy, in the middle of "I'm Sorry" by Brenda Lee, burst out with a question that had been on nobody's list, a question she did not even know she wanted the answer to. "Mama--can I ask you something about back when?"

Susie looked a bit surprised, but then nodded.

"What were all those cucumber clippings about?" Maggie gave her a look that said "Why are you asking that???" and Cammy returned that look with one that said "No idea."

Susie closed her eyes, and then opened them. She

hesitated before answering, inspecting her daughters as if assessing whether they were old enough to hear this. But of course they were--they were almost old ladies like herself! Good grief--what had happened to them all? Well, no sense holding anything back now. She took a breath and said, remembering the whole cucumber incident, "I discovered that a cucumber is a pretty good substitute for a penis, and your dad caught me in the act. I wasn't ashamed, but he shamed me for it. He never let me forget that it humiliated him. But girls, let me tell you something--sometimes a woman has to do things to ensure her own satisfaction, if her man won't. And that's all I'm going to say."

Maggie and Cammy were too stunned to say anything either, so for the next several miles there was silence in the van. Cammy, however, had to pursue it. "But then it stopped. Did he forgive you?"

A little smile played along Susie's lips as she recalled the cucumber's replacement. "I guess in a way he did. I let him think he was satisfying me, because I had gotten something better than a cucumber. Thanks to Connie. I miss Connie so much."

The sisters had ever so many more questions at that point. What was better than the cucumber? And how had Connie been involved? They wanted to know everything, but the playlist had ended, and Susie began to drift away. She stared out the window and asked politely, "Where are we going again?"

Chapter Thirty-six
1960

Susie went back to teaching with zeal, but her wifely attitude did not improve all that much. If holding a grudge were a sport, Susie would be a world champion. She was definitely still angry at Bud for what he had done, and more so because of all the anguish it had caused her, mentally, emotionally, and physically. She had periods where she was overcome with grief, followed by relief, followed by guilt. She continued to sleep in the marital bed but refused to engage in sex with him.

One night, in desperation, Bud decided to try what Connie had recommended. When they were both settled in the bed and he judged Susie was nearly asleep, he crept under the covers and put his head between her legs. She jerked awake but remained still. This was interesting. She wanted to see what would happen. He proceeded to do the thing that Connie had whispered to her about that day in the teacher's lounge, and it was beyond amazing. She was fully his, she would do anything he wished, if only this would continue. However, that was not to be. Bud was still not in favor of what he considered illegitimate methods of stimulation. Also, in his mind, that sort of thing was dirty, was what you did with back street girls, not the woman you cherish. That night was wonderful but the next time they made love, it was back to the old ways. Susie was so disappointed. When she tried to initiate it again, they got into an argument about it. Over the next few months it developed into an issue between them. She wondered where he had learned that, and didn't understand why he would not repeat it. She guessed she would go back to withholding then, if that's the way things were going to be. At least she still had her BOB.

She became alert to his comings and goings, suspecting a possible affair. He was, in fact, traveling more now with work. Holiday Inns were popping up all over the place, and he was the inspector general, as it were, of the finished product, making sure that each one was up to the standards in all respects. She began examining his laundry when he returned from a trip, looking for the telltale "lipstick on his collar."

Meanwhile, in current events, something Susie included in her fourth-grade curriculum because she thought it vitally important, the presidential campaign was heating up. It was one of the big "firsts," you could say. A Catholic running for President. An Irish Catholic, no less. John Fitzgerald Kennedy. Susie's dad would have been so proud. She couldn't wait to vote for him--and he was so handsome! Bud, it turned out, had a hidden streak of prejudice in him against Catholics, apparently. He intended to vote for Nixon. Susie could not understand this for all the world, and it distressed her greatly. They argued about it a lot. Susie was not one to shy away from making waves. She believed in being clear about things.

Also in the current events department, Bud was keeping an eye on the whole Vietnam thing, which was becoming worrisome. The first U.S. "advisors" had been killed last year. Somehow the Chinese communism was more threatening than the Japanese imperialism in Korea a few years ago. Bud was seriously considering signing up if this turned into an all-out war. Domino theory. He talked about that possibility with Susie. She of course was adamantly against it. Hadn't he endured enough suffering in the other war he was in? And what about his family? What were they supposed to do?

Bud was accumulating a lot of negative tally marks in the scoresheet of marital considerations. Of course, he hadn't had any in the beginning. Although, what do two people really know about each other before they marry? Not all that much. Marriage is a process of learning and adjusting expectations (or not), also adjusting behavior (or not), compromising, and listening to learn (or not). Little things can drive one nuts after a while, if allowed to. The way he says "Oh Jeez" every single time after a sneeze, those things that are more predictable than gravity, can turn on a person and become like poison darts.

Chapter Thirty-seven

Home at last! Maggie pulled into her driveway and heaved a big sigh of relief. She jumped out of the car and went around to open the door for Susie. Cammy was still sitting in the passenger seat playing on her phone.

"Earth to Cammy--we're here!" Maggie announced.

"I know--just a sec. I'm about to win this level."

Maggie rolled her eyes. "What is so important about that stupid game?" she asked in exasperation.

"I know, it's disgusting that I'm so addicted. But it doesn't hurt anyone. And I have learned some life lessons from it, believe it or not."

"Oh really. Like what?" Maggie asked, as she helped Susie out of the van.

"Like, if you just have patience and persist in what you're doing, you will eventually win. I know they are always trying to get you to spend money and buy more lives or what-have-you, but I never do. I can outlast them. It's like what Dad--er, Bud used to say to me sometimes when I would get the doldrums. I can't remember the Latin, he said it in Latin--but it was a phrase he said he learned in the war; it means 'don't let the bastards grind you down.'"

"Illegitimis non carborundum," they heard from Susie's mouth. At which they turned and stared at her. She was obviously tracking perfectly at this moment.

"Yes--that was it. I think he even had a desk plaque at work with those words on it."

"I gave him that one year for his birthday," Susie said, with a look of fond remembrance. "It's not really a bona fide Latin phrase--it's not strictly correct, but it got started and then went wild." She looked then right at Cammy and said, "And did it help you, that advice?"

Cammy had to stop and think a minute. "I guess so. At any rate, I didn't kill myself."

At that point Susie looked at both of them with such love and grief. "Tell me everything," she said. "I want to know how bad it was. And I want you to know how deeply sorry I am."

"Well," said Maggie, "we're not going to do that right here in my driveway. Let's get settled in the house first, maybe have a bite to eat and something to drink." She was thinking of a stiff shot of whiskey herself.

Of course there was no food in the house, since no one had been there for almost two weeks, so then Maggie had to run to the store before they closed--it had been dark dusk when they pulled in, and her local grocery closed at eight. She left Cammy with instructions to show Susie to her room--a guest room that had not been expecting this new occupant and thus was in need of "tidying up." Meaning it was the room where Maggie stashed piles of mail, purchases she had not yet escorted to their intended destination, books she had picked up to resell; everything that would look untidy in the main rooms gathered here in concentrated untidiness. Cammy took one look in there and backed out, shaking her head. No way would she install Susie there--there was no room even for one suitcase, let alone all the other things they had brought in the van. She guided Susie back to the living room, got each of them a glass of water, and they sat down in comfortable leather chairs.

"She has another room upstairs that's bigger and nicer," said Cammy. "That room in there is too messy and full of her stuff. We... uh, we didn't realize you would be coming here actually, so nothing's been..."

"I know, I know," Susie cut in. "I know this is the most awkward thing that ever was, but I can't..." her voice staggered and changed. "I can't... think what else to do." She was on the verge of total distress, it appeared, grasping at the lucidity that was already escaping her even as she moaned out her words. The brand new environment sucked out the clarity she had expressed just moments ago in the driveway.

Cammy felt her heart crack. The nurse in her, the parent in her felt such love and empathy for this person, and there was no holding back because of professional guidelines--after all it was her own mother--her *mother!*

"Oh Mama!" she cried. "It doesn't matter. Of course you should come back here!" She lurched ungracefully over to Susie's chair and leaned down to hug her. Susie's head was in her hands in despair, so it was more of a one-armed side hug at the last minute. "Everything will be fine--you'll see. It'll be fine. Please don't worry about it."

"Really?" Susie looked up hopefully at Cammy, her face considering a smile, eyes desperate for reassurance.

"I promise," said Cammy, and they moved over to the

couch and sat together and held hands. Cammy turned on the TV. Susie sighed and was quite content.

Maggie returned with rotisserie chicken and deli salads, and while they ate dinner they figured out which room Susie could have. The nicer room involved going up and down a set of stairs, but after some discussion they all agreed that Susie could still handle stairs. So that was settled, the necessary stuff was brought in from the van, and between them the sisters got Susie put to bed upstairs. There was no long talk reminiscing about just how bad it had been.

Back downstairs, Maggie said, "I guess I could clear off at least one bed in this guest room for you to sleep in."

"You know, I think I'll just head on over to Da--I mean Bud's and check on things there. I haven't heard from Matthew for a couple of days."

Maggie nodded, considering. "I guess we're going to have some change around here, now there's both of them to attend to."

"I already figured that out, sister. Well, she's at your house, that's all I'm going to say for now. We'll just have to see what develops."

"So now I'm the caregiver, 24-7, is that what we're saying here?"

"No, no no. We will look into residential options, memory care centers, you know--all the usual things. At least adult day care respite programs, home caregivers. Hell, maybe even Viola or Esther have some shifts open--ha! I'll ask tomorrow. I might spend the night there instead of going home. I don't know--depends how things are there. Did I tell you about the drawerful of Mama's school pictures?"

Maggie nodded. "Yes. That's a little bit creepy, don't you think? I mean, that he saved all those whenever anyone would find one over the years? I remember Mrs. Wise found one when she went to make us a pie or cake or something, and there was one taped to the inside of the flour canister lid. She kinda jumped at first but then calmly took it out and dusted it off. She always had a soft spot for Mama." But Cammy did not remember this.

Chapter Thirty-eight

Spring 1960

As a final project in her fourth-grade class, Susie assigned her students an in-depth report on another country or city. It was really a research paper, in an effort to teach them how to use the library and reference books. They even had to establish contact with a student in that place and become pen pals with them. Of course she helped with letter-writing instruction and suggestions of tools, addresses to write to, and so on. But she was very demanding, and they had to do a lot of work themselves, not just copy an encyclopedia entry.

That year one student--Clara in fact, Maggie's friend who had complained about the substitute teacher--wrote her paper about Nova Scotia. Clara's mother was deeply into genealogy, and was aware that a Scottish ancestor had been one of the founding members in a brief Scottish colonization of Nova Scotia. She wanted to pass on her enthusiasm for personal history to Clara, and so she practically wrote the report for her. It leaned rather heavily on family lore, but Clara managed to include enough facts about climate, cities, economics, and government to satisfy Mrs. Benson. And then her mother was able, through a distant relation, to get the name of a teacher in an elementary school. Being a little shy, Clara did not know how to write to the teacher and ask for a pen pal. But she figured Mrs. Benson would. So Mrs. Benson wrote to Don, her future husband, asking for a pen pal for one of her students in a study of Nova Scotia.

At first it was just a series of random, polite, friendly little notes, checking in on the project. But they discovered fairly soon that they enjoyed discussing teaching, and the letters got longer. They could share tips and ideas they had been successful with, and debate trends in education. Neither of their spouses were able to fill that need for them, not being teachers themselves. Bud had very little actual tolerance for Susie going into detail about her teaching life. His eyes would glaze over and then he would come up with a reason he had to attend to something else right then.

Gradually the letters began to include little bits of personal information. They each had two children, his younger than hers, very young in fact. He was finding it hard to get enough sleep. Susie rolled her inner eyes at that. Ha, she thought. Try being the mother. Eventually she disclosed pretty much all her dissatisfaction with various situations in her marriage--well not the sex part, but everything else, including the bomb shelter and the punctured condom and the miscarriage. That was pretty personal, but Susie was desperate for a companionable person. Connie had moved back to New Jersey suddenly when her husband's unit got called up to go hang about in the South China Sea, and Susie missed her dearly. Missed having someone to complain to about Bud. So she kind of transferred that role to Don. For his part, Don, it turned out, was seeing a new side of his wife, as a parent of two little ones, and he wasn't so sure he liked what he saw. Susie could relate, only she was feeling empathy for his wife. She tried to explain to him a few things about how hard that was, from her own experience--how you're just so tired all the time, and there aren't enough hours in the day to do all the things you normally would have done AND take care of two babies. It's hard to even find time to shower, for heaven's sake. He said he was so touched by that, that she truly helped him to be more understanding, and thanked her in wonderment for taking the time and trouble to reach out personally to him. So really, at first Susie strengthened Don's marriage.

After several weeks of frequent letter writing, Susie found herself looking forward to getting a letter from Don more than anything else in her life. Oh, the kids were fine, but all she and Bud ever did was argue lately. She fell into a habit of making Don the confidante that Connie had been, the one who she could share the latest outrage with. Could Don believe that Bud was now talking about going back on active duty in case a war should break out in Vietnam? At that, Don was appalled, because after all, the man has a family to support. That's exactly what Susie thought too. They would chat about their classrooms and students, and the research papers her class was assigned. She asked him about all the interesting facts she had learned from Clara's report. Was he by any chance descended from those Scots? They were so compatible. Susie wondered if she possibly had any Scotch ancestry from there. She knew next to nothing about her ancestry.

And then one day a letter came, after several days with

none (they had begun to write almost every day). Don's wife, Delores, had been diagnosed with breast cancer. He might not have time to write so often, since he would be working and then doing more parent time while she went through treatment, which was to start immediately. Oh God, thought Susie. Oh no. Poor Don. She didn't think 'poor Delores' by this time, but 'poor Don.' She said she understood of course, and wished him good luck, and please let her know if there was anything she could do to help--although she wondered what that could ever be. In a week, there was another letter. Could he possibly get a phone number for her, and they could just talk instead of writing? So she told him a way to call her at school, to the phone in the teacher's lounge. If he could call about three o'clock her time, school would just be over, and no one would be in the teacher's lounge. It would be private.

The first time he called, she was there waiting. It came at 3:10. Don was at home, in his kitchen, watching his two boys play in the living room. Delores was in the hospital. She was due to have a radical mastectomy the next morning. Don was trying to bear up, but there was so much. School was nearly out for the summer, and he had report cards to do, she knew what that was like. She did know what that was like, since her school was also about to end, and she had her own report cards to do, though she didn't complain about it. Don did rather love to complain, if he could be said to have a fault or two.

The next day he called again at the same time. The surgery had gone well enough, he supposed. A friend had watched the children while he waited at the hospital. He hated that he had to have a substitute right at the end of school, and was hoping he could go back for at least the last day. He was having to do the report cards at home, after he got the kids in bed. Susie nodded, closed her eyes, and pictured him--sitting at his kitchen table, overhead light blaring down, perhaps a late-night cup of coffee in his hand, mulling over the children he served. Or did he perhaps have a real desk, maybe a roll-top, and did he sit there in a nice set of loungewear, a smoking jacket draped around his shoulders? No, not that. Don was definitely way more proletariat than that. She realized then that she wanted to know everything about him and his life, and something stirred in her nether region. Something she had not felt for a long time now, it seemed to her.

They had to figure out a way to keep calling for the summer, since Susie's school was now out for summer vacation (she had two days to clean up her classroom, so she could still take this call, but after that, nothing). Also Don would be home caring for an ill and disabled wife and two small children. How could they talk every day? Susie came to the shocking revelation that they were behaving exactly like two people who were having an affair.

She brought them face to face with that. "Look at us--ha ha! You would think we were having an affair!"

"It does appear that way," acknowledged Don. "But of course that's ridiculous. Isn't it?"

They agreed that it would be best if they went back to writing letters. But they would write every day, they pledged.

Chapter Thirty-nine

When Cammy got to Bud's house it was pretty late, and all the lights were out. She didn't want to disturb anyone if it wasn't necessary, so she went on home to her house. Dean was still up, very glad to see her, and spent the next two hours listening to her tales of adventure in Nova Scotia, revelations and discoveries--Flower, her mother's hooked rug artwork, Ted and Michael and their families, poutine (!), and on and on until they both ran out of steam and succumbed to a deep and peaceful sleep.

The next morning, feeling refreshed and ready to face the tasks she had outlined to Maggie last night, and happy to have her own morning routine back--coffee, news check, and a few rounds of Candy Crush--Cammy got in the car and drove to Bud's.

Letting herself in the back door, she greeted Viola, who was already there preparing lunch and throwing in a load of laundry. Bud and Matthew were sitting in the den, watching TV. When Cammy went in there she almost didn't recognize her father. He looked so much older, haggard and vacant.

Her surprise and alarm must have showed in her face because Matthew said, "Mom! Hi! We didn't know you were home--what's wrong?"

"Wrong? Nothing's wrong with me. Is everything

all right here?" She inclined her head toward Bud, who hadn't seemed to notice her entrance.

Matthew got up, went over, and hugged his mom. "Does he seem a lot different to you? He hasn't really been very good ever since those two incidents with the pictures. Pretty out of it most days. But we maintain the routines exactly--that helps get us and him through the days." Matthew was sounding like an experienced caregiver, and Cammy wondered if he was going to be happy to be relieved of his duties now that she was back. He answered her unspoken question before she could answer it. "Actually, Mom, I kinda like doing this. I was thinking, what if I just started staying here instead of at home? I could be the night time helper, and in case anything happened in the middle of the night again, someone would be here."

She was again amazed by and proud of her son. She had to admit that it was an ideal solution for now. "But that sounds like a job, Matt. I don't know if there's enough funds to pay you for that."

"Fine, let's just think it over, and see what happens. For now, I'll just keep on without pay, okay?" He glanced toward the hallway, where Viola was lingering, obviously listening to their conversation. They exchanged a look, and she moved on.

"Well, if you're sure," Cammy said dubiously, wondering what kind of look that was that passed between Matthew and Viola. "I would sure like to have a little time off from this."

Viola was a forty-something single mother of two teenagers, Derell and Tanya. She actually lived in south Memphis, not far from where Cammy and Dean and Matthew lived, which was discovered one day while Matthew was staying at Bud's. She had come to work that day without her car, having let her son use it--it was a day of no school, so Derell had driven her to her job, and then taken the car to get to a job interview. When it was time for her shift to be over, she was going to have to wait for him to pick her up. Matthew offered to drive her home--he wanted to stop by his house and pick up some clean clothes anyway, and when he found out where she lived, he insisted on taking her. Along the way they chatted, and discovered that they had more in common than one would have thought, being near the same age and thus having lived through common cultural trends and so forth. Her neighborhood looked much like his own, one of so many in the city filled with red brick homes.

Since that day, Matthew had made a point of casually hanging out in the kitchen whenever it was Viola's shift, and visiting with her. They found much to laugh about, and he considered her to be almost as skillful as Esther when it came to dealing with Bud. Also, she was quite attractive, with beautiful chestnut brown skin and poochy lips, high cheekbones, shiny black hair worn in a natural bun and, usually, large hoop earrings. She was sassy in a pleasant but no-nonsense way.

Meanwhile, at Maggie's, Susie was up very early, wandering around in a fog, examining all the rooms, all the furniture, the knick-knacks, the artwork on the walls. She bumped into a low dormer ceiling with a loud thump, which woke Maggie up.

"Mama? Are you okay?" Maggie hurried out into the hall from her bedroom.

"Where am I?" Susie was totally bewildered.

"Why, you're in my house, Mama. You've never been here before, so it will take a while for you to get used to it probably," she said, putting one arm around Susie.

"But I want to go home," she whined.

Maggie, and this was before coffee, had to stop and give herself some time to think about that one. Home? The one they had just recently left after parsing it all out? Could she be wanting to go back to that one?

"What home, Mama?" She decided to see what Susie would say if she asked, even though it probably wouldn't make sense. But it might. Meanwhile she took Susie's arm and guided her down the stairs, aiming for the kitchen. "Let's fix us some breakfast, what do you say? I had the presence of mind last night to get supplies for this morning, though I'll have to go back for a lot more groceries later today, I think." As she said those words, she realized, like a mother with a first child, that she could not just run to the store or anywhere anymore without taking Susie with her. Whew--this was really going to be cumbersome. They would have to get started looking for caregivers to come in right away. She would call Cammy after they ate breakfast. "What do you like to eat for breakfast, Mama?" Maggie asked. But Susie was sitting in the breakfast nook at the table, just looking at everything in confusion.

Cammy decided she had better stay at Bud's for at least long enough to reestablish his acquaintance, as it were, make sure he still knew who she was, after she was gone so long. Also, he apparently had a regression of some sort, or progression really, if she were honest about the course of the disease. So she sat down with him on the couch and tried her best to make some conversation. Matthew looked on for a bit, then went into the kitchen to "see if Viola needs any help" getting lunch on. Cammy raised her internal eyebrows so high at this it was a wonder her glasses didn't fall off their place on her head. This was a development she had never witnessed firsthand--Matthew's interest in a particular woman. Oh he had had a few girlfriends over the years, but eventually driven them away as his behavior graduated from quirky to crazy. What, she wondered, would this turn into, if anything? She had long ago given up hoping for him to have a "normal" relationship, or that she would ever have grandchildren.

Cammy became so engrossed with her thoughts about this, and with trying to get Bud back to some lucidity, that she completely forgot about Maggie and Susie out there in Collierville. Finally, around dinnertime, Maggie called.

"Where are you?? I've waited all day for you to come and help me decide on some caregiving, or make calls or something--at least spell me yourself. I never even made it to the store! Now we have nothing for dinner!"

"Oh my God--I'm so sorry Mags! I got involved with things here. Bud doesn't even know who I am anymore. And there's an interesting development with Matthew and Viola that I can't wait to tell you about." One thing Maggie and Cammy had always enjoyed together was gossip. Or "people perimeter check," as they preferred to call it when they got old enough to know what that meant. "Why don't you order in a pizza, get a good night's sleep, and then I'll come out first thing in the morning? How is she today, by the way?"

"She's awful--same as Daddy it sounds like. She's confused, has no idea where she is, and keeps saying she wants to go home!"

"Oh lord. Here we go. Buckle up, boys and girls."

The pizza revived Susie somewhat--she had always loved pizza, and this was a good one, the kind she liked, with a thin cracker crust. She seemed then to perk up and attempt some chattiness with Maggie, but she was time-traveling. At length they settled into just watching Jeopardy! and Wheel of Fortune, with occasional shout-outs of answers. Maggie and Mama had always liked to see which one could guess it first--they were a little competitive that way.

After she got Susie to bed at a fairly decent hour,

Maggie stayed up watching late night TV for comic relief and reality check on the news of the day. She opened a can of mixed nuts and watched an episode of a show she was following on Netflix, popping the yummy salted almonds and sipping a little bourbon. It was good to be in her own home at least. Home--what was that for Susie? She lit up a joint she had stashed under the coffee table, to make her sleepy. Got lost in deep thoughts and memories until an even later hour. When she finally went to bed, her insides felt like a clockworks--little tiny gears churning away, things thumping, her pulse was fast, her tongue was prickly from all that salt, then big boluses would move inside her, then a pinprick sharp itch on her outer left vulva, then a sudden chest pain under the rib nearest her heart. A feeling in one nostril that perhaps a nosebleed was starting. Was she having a stroke? Oh, that would be the icing on the cake, wouldn't it? But, she took some deep breaths and knew that if she just waited it out, eventually she would fall asleep and feel normal the next morning. And that is what happened.

Cammy came over as promised, and Maggie went off to shop first thing, before any other emergency could prevent her. Ah, another bit of normalcy--the grocery store! Maggie loved shopping of all kinds. She took her time wandering up and down every aisle, as she had no list. Operating without a net, she called it. Her cart filled up with cans and boxes, Styrofoam trays wrapped with plastic, and cartons of milk and juice. As she meandered in the produce section, her eye fell upon the organic cucumbers, which were not all smooth and straight like the non-organic ones. One of them put her in mind of Susie's comment about the cucumber incident back when. She paused, picked it up, hefted it in her hand, and considered. It had been a while. Maggie had pretty much given up on men about twenty-five years ago, decided it wasn't worth it, and stopped doing things to meet men. She went with a girlfriend when she wanted to go to a movie or out to dinner. She lived a chaste life in many respects. What the hell, she thought, and tossed it in her basket.

Chapter Forty

Summer 1960

Now that Mama had no work to occupy her mind, since school was out for the summer vacation, she was irritable, restless. She smoked a lot, but refused to go out onto the porch, from where the bomb shelter was visible. She was eternally boycotting the backyard, and so the house began to smell like stale cigarette smoke. But it was clean: Mama was constantly scrubbing, vacuuming, doing dishes. They had gotten a new appliance, an automatic dishwasher; it was actually kind of fun to load dirty dishes and unload clean dishes--almost magic! She didn't want to go anywhere, would not take them to the pool, or even go shopping. She was just waiting, it seemed to the girls, all morning for the mail to come, and then after asking repeatedly if it was there yet, insisting on getting it herself. There would always be a letter. When they asked her who it was that was writing to her every day, she ignored the question. Because of course they noticed--at least Cammy, back to being hypervigilant to the emotional barometer of the house, did. And she was not averse to asking aloud what it meant.

Daddy, it seemed, was having to go out of town practically every week, sometimes for several days at a time, for his job with Holiday Inn. That was really better, the girls agreed, because when he was home, they just argued.

They argued about politics--the upcoming election was much in the news; they argued about whether if Vietnam turned into a war, Bud should sign up for duty; and they argued because (and this part was unbeknownst to the children) they had not had sex in months. Daddy never saw any of the letters. Cammy never did either, though she wondered where Mama stashed them after each day's arrival. There must be a big stack of them somewhere, she reasoned. It crossed her mind to snoop around until she found them, but, careful rule-follower that she was, she never did. Daddy was promising to take them to New York again in September for her birthday--this was becoming a tradition!--and she didn't want to wreck the chances of that. *Bye Bye Birdie* was on Broadway, and he said he would take them to see that. They had actually seen it in Memphis when a local theater produced it, and she had loved it so much! She was dying to see the real thing on Broadway! Of course he was also planning on taking them to see the Howdy Doody Show again, which Cammy felt she was a little too old for, but she supposed Maggie would still enjoy it.

Each day after the mail finally came, Mama's mood would change; she would relax and they would all go to the pool at the country club, where they got to order Shirley Temples, and sip them by the pool. The girls would splash and play in the water, practicing hand-stands on the bottom, practicing their diving off the side of the deep end and off the low board ("Mama! Look at this one Mama--watch me!"), and Mama would sit on a chaise lounge under an umbrella (nodding, "Oh yes--that's a great one. Mm-hmm") and write a letter back, presumably, to the one who wrote her every day. Cammy's mind, filled with Nancy Drew notions, imagined all kinds of scenarios, which she shared with Maggie, though Maggie seemed to be trying her best to be oblivious to it all. She was nine--she just wanted to go outside and play horses with her neighborhood friend. They were both collecting horses, and they sometimes combined their various steeds and riders for a richly imagined story. It could engross them for hours a day.

In mid-August, just as school was about to begin again (schools in the south start well before September), the letters stopped coming. Susie was visibly upset the first day, and every day as it went on, she got worse. But since she was at school setting up her classroom, at least she could focus on prep. And she took advantage of that fact to write to Don a very short letter: "What's wrong? Call me. Back at school." Thereafter she waited in the teacher's lounge until the call came. It was bad news. Delores' cancer had spread; there was nothing more to do except get her affairs in order. He had been preoccupied with all of that, plus of course taking care of the boys and trying to plan for his school year. He sounded so tired, and so sad. Her heart went out to him, and she wanted nothing more than to do something to help him. He said they were going to take one last trip together while they still could. Delores wanted to go up to Cape Breton Island and hear Celtic music and some Gaelic speaking, which was dying out slowly--only several thousand speakers were left. They would be tourists up there for a week, then Don was going to come home and return to his classroom, while Delores would make one last visit to her parents over in Londonderry, to say goodbye. She would take the children with her if she possibly could--she had missed them so much while being unable to care for them. And they didn't get to see their grandparents often. But first she had to rest and recuperate a bit from the treatment's side effects, before she would even feel up to going.

Susie's mind was calculating, thinking of her family's upcoming visit to New York. "So, when do you think that might be, that you leave? Any idea?"

"None. We'll just have to see how she feels, if she does even start to feel better. I hope we get to."

"Of course you do. So do I, for your sake. I was just thinking… oh never mind."

"No, what? Please tell me."

"Ah, I was imagining that I could take a trip out there. While she's at her parents' place."

"What?" Don was clearly shocked. "Are you serious? Because I had never… I mean, no, I really couldn't do something like that." He was practically sputtering.

"As a friend. To help you out, so you could concentrate on school. I could be the wife while she's not there--wait no--that's not what I meant. I meant just cooking and cleaning and laundry and stuff like that. Never mind. Forget I said anything like that."

"What about your own family? How could that work?"

She told him about the annual trip to New York for Cammy's birthday present, and how she would be home alone for at least a week, maybe more. She could just go away and no one would be any the wiser.

And just like that did the unthinkable become thinkable.

Chapter Forty-one

"We have to find a doctor for her, first off," said Cammy to Maggie three mornings after they were back in Memphis. "I don't even know what kind of meds she's on, if any. We should have thought of having her medical records transferred, but we wouldn't have known where to send them anyway, because… no doctor."

"Let's get Meghan on that," joked Maggie, but then realized it wasn't really a joke. They would have to enlist the help of the Canadians, as they had come to call the lot of them. "In fact, why didn't they discuss her meds with us when we were there? They had more time to think things through, in my opinion. They should have prioritized this. What kind of doctor should we get? A neurologist? A cardiologist? I could hold my nose and call Jim P. and get a referral to a good one--not him," she said, referring to her ex-husband.

"I was thinking of a gerontologist," said Cammy. "Specializing in the aged. That might cover most of her deals, whatever they are. And did the Alert lifeline thing come with us? Or do we have to get a new one set up here? How are we going to monitor her for the falling? Will she need to have a person with her constantly?"

They were sitting in Maggie's breakfast nook, having coffee and pastries, and they were not having to watch

Mama because Cammy had brought Matthew (and Viola) over to meet Susie. They were in the living room getting to know each other. Susie kind of knew who Matthew was, but was confused about where exactly she was. Viola was being considered for and considering some shifts as caregiver, if it seemed a good fit. She was perhaps waiting and watching Matthew with Susie before making up her mind; she held back, didn't say much, which was not really her usual style. She could use the work, but if it was going to complicate the family situation, which suddenly seemed to have gotten way more complicated already, she might not take it. Where was Matthew going to hang out, she wondered. Was he even going to still be at Bud's, now that Cammy was back? Were the sisters intending to transfer him over here to Maggie's to be his grandma's companion? As if he was a toy soldier they could move about at their will, she thought. He's a grown man--he can do what he wants. But if he was here, she might definitely take some shifts here. Viola knew from her new friendship with Matthew that he did not want to go back to Cammy and Dean's house again. She supposed this could be another room and board kind of job for Matthew, but she really thought what he needed was a paying job, to bring up his self-esteem. She had mentioned to him that he should take the course to become a certified caregiver and get some other jobs in the expanding field--there was a booming need for caregivers. He said he would think about it, which means nothing at all. But she pointed out all that he had learned in being with Bud--he had learned how to handle all kinds of situations, could easily do the physical things (he was in pretty good shape), and furthermore he had a kind heart and loving approach. Private caregiver jobs paid pretty well, she also pointed out. It wasn't so great if you worked through an agency that got government contracts--then you absolutely had to be certified, plus the pay was shit. But there were still lots of private jobs out there. Hers, for instance, at Bud's. After a long career with Holiday Inn, Bud had enough money stashed away to be able to afford private helpers. Matthew had nodded. He hadn't really given much thought to the caregivers' pay or the source of it.

Bud, in fact, had lots of money and other assets, a result of his having risen up through the ranks with Holiday Inn. The company had become the absolute leader in the field, setting the standards that the other major hotel chains--Ramada Inn, Quality Inn, Best Western, and Howard Johnson's--tried to emulate. And then it had introduced game-changing technology that put them way ahead--the 1-800 toll-free telephone number! In the 1960's, they opened a chain of campgrounds, Holiday Inn Trav-L Park system. This was a challenging period for Bud and the girls. He was in charge of these campgrounds, and got on a big campaign of going to each one and camping. They, of course, were teenage girls, in Memphis, and not that interested in camping. Oh they had gone, because... they were all trying to keep up the illusion that they were a family. They were afraid to go against him too much for his sake, not their own, though of course, as teenage girls, there was some rebellion. Yet, if they were totally honest, some of their best memories came from then. Sometimes they were allowed to ask a friend to go camping with them, and as most of the campgrounds were actually on beautiful bits of land, often on a lake or a river, they had enjoyed all the things--the boating, the skiing, the s'mores over the campfire. It was fun. It was just that sometimes it conflicted with other activities they wished to be involved in, and the camping always won.

In 1967 Holiday Inn opened its 1-800 toll-free call center. Cammy was nineteen, and got her first job there. It was supposed to be just a summer job, between her freshman and sophomore year at Memphis State, but it turned out to be more than that. She found she liked it--liked doing the work and making her own money, liked having something to think about that crowded out the humiliation and shame and heartbreak that she lived with for the last seven years. So she stayed at the job full-time, and took night classes in pre-nursing at Memphis State. This arrangement lasted throughout the duration of her education and medical training.

Four years later, Holiday Inn opened a training facility--Holiday Inn University and Conference Center, in Olive Branch, Mississippi, just south of Memphis. Bud was asked to be a "dean" of the university, and spent most of his time down there, only coming home on the weekends. Cammy was by this time working as a nurse, and engaged to Dean, so she was hardly ever home. Maggie had the place pretty much to herself all week.

She was twenty-one. This was her wild period--she and her future husband the cardiologist were partying hard.

And then Holiday Inn opened a whole airport at Olive Branch for company aircraft. Bud took classes and training, then applied for and received his pilot's license, and presto! He was able to fly a small Learjet by himself to whichever inn he was going to for inspection. It gave him a feeling of power, and it must be said, he cut a very dashing figure to those employees sent to fetch him in a car as he stepped out of the plane, with his shock of white hair and his handsome face. More than a few female heads were turned. Even though Bud never remarried, he was not without women companions at regular intervals. But a relationship would only get so far before they came to the point of realizing that Bud was a heartbroken man and yearned for only one woman.

Even after Kemmons Wilson left the company, and they decided to scrap the Great Sign for a cheaper one, which signaled the receding of the Holiday Inn brand, Bud continued to earn a very good living from the many tentacled endeavors they had entwined with--Gulf Oil, Continental Trailways Bus Company, the Delta Queen, nursing homes, a television production company that made syndicated country music shows, and various spin-off corporations. He had wise investment advice, and prospered. Not that he spent much of it--his Scotch ancestry asserted itself somewhat when not tempered by a less frugal partner. So he had enough to sustain him in style for this, his old-age infirmity.

One time, though, many years ago now, he did decide

to spend some money. He had been sitting out on the porch, sipping some whiskey and smoking a cigar--cigars were all the rage at that point--when his gaze fell upon the old bomb shelter, now overgrown with weeds and brambles of all kinds, looking a bit like a sod house. Suddenly he was seized with regret and sadness, the recognition, perhaps, that his insistence on building that was one of the first cracks in his marriage. How could he have done that to the woman he adored? Of course the cold war was long over, the threat of nuclear disaster being just a distant memory. So--he called up a construction crew the next morning, and within the week the bomb shelter was once again a greenhouse. When he proudly showed it to his daughters, as he saw them both pretty often, they were struck with emotional shrapnel, but mainly heartbreak for him, Bud. Why could he not move on, they wondered. They each felt like they had made their peace with Mama leaving as best they could (of course they had the advantage of seeing or hearing from her once in a while). But Bud was stuck, forever it seemed, on Susie. Since there was no one to work in it or plant a garden, it had inevitably gotten buried in brush again after several years, and there it stood today, a visual symbol of his lifelong love, weather-beaten and abandoned.

Cammy was making notes of all the questions they had, all the things on their to-do list, which was getting longer by the minute. They had to establish power of attorney, they should probably--no definitely--think about end-of-life issues, directives on care in case of inability to communicate, which they realized was pretty much now, at times. They had to try and have that talk with Mama though, to know her ideas and desires if possible. That should be interesting, thought Cammy. She might ask Esther, who seemed to be somewhat experienced in these things, if she could help. They had done it for Bud, when he first started having signs of Alzheimer's, before the disease had progressed too far.

Matthew was thinking about the way Viola had talked to him about getting work. It was in a very flirtatious way, as if promising something more than friendship if he did. He wondered if he was ready to take another run at living a "normal" life out in the world, instead of hiding away in his parents' home. Did he have whatever it was that enabled most people to do that? Or was his brain hopelessly broken? What was a "mental" illness, and is there a cure? Besides all these pills he has to take? Is it all just chemistry? He thought about Viola--her situation, her two teenage children, the color of her skin (because in Memphis, that must needs be thought about). And then he thought about her full lips and high cheekbones, and the way her breasts stood up all perky when she wore something a little clingy, and he thought perhaps he could give it a try. The song lyric "Have a little faith in me" ran through his mind. He might try having some faith in himself.

Chapter Forty-two

With the Scorpio Season Guide in the back of her mind, Maggie was ever alert for opportunities to check off the final three recommendations, or guidelines. Right now she was thinking of

"Identify where your greatest
power comes from."

She was looking at *A Wrinkle in Time* and wondering what it might bring, and whether to write to this person or call this other person, deciding on her best approach. And really, that was her best power, trading up for greater "value" in the currency of books. She was better at that than any other careers she had tried, especially her interior design phase--that had been a dismal failure. So yes, she should just admit that this was her best power and go for it. Somewhat troubling was the niggling thought that perhaps 'greatest power' was not congruent with 'best power' in the sense that she used, but more of a source question. Maggie was not much of a higher source believer and always tended to go with the worldly rather than the spiritual, which begs the question of why she was following the astrological guidelines so assiduously, but there you have the crux of humanity's dilemma--paradoxical contradictions.

Nevertheless, when she got down to work on it, she had a very satisfying number to look at. $10,500, to be exact. This was an extraordinarily big success for Maggie--definitely one of her biggest ever. She felt like celebrating with someone, but who? Who really cared about what she did? Mama might not even comprehend; Cammy might, but she had taken Mama to her first doctor's appointment, so Maggie had some alone time. Well, it would just have to be a solitary celebration. Since it was after lunch, she allowed herself a glass of white wine and turned on the TV--she could watch one of her shows. Having finished one series and being between things, she was weighing going back and rewatching "Six Feet Under" or starting "Orange is the New Black." She opted for the latter. The very first episode showed Maggie such a shocking and arousing sex scene that she had to retire to her room with the cucumber to consummate the viewing. Oh my, yes, there was a definite appeal to the cucumber--Maggie had to agree with Susie there. Plus it was completely flexible and amenable to suggestions. Oh, this was lovely. And it achieved the added bonus of the second to last checkoff:

"Reconnect with the erotic."

Chapter Forty-three

The gerontologist had given Cammy a lot of paperwork to fill out, and Susie's health history, as far as she knew it, while Susie was occupied by the nurse taking all of her basic information, weight, blood pressure, etc. Cammy found she knew so very little it was embarrassing. The doctor started looking at her funny, when she had to leave so many questions unanswered, and Cammy had to explain that her mother had moved away to Nova Scotia and lived there for the past umpty-ump years until just now, when she had returned to Memphis to be cared for in her decrepitude by the daughters she abandoned in pre-adolescence. That all came out with more attitude than she intended--the doctor raised one eyebrow. Cammy ignored that and plunged on, telling her what she had learned in Nova Scotia, and the falling, and all about the Jamaicans.

Dr. Mary was very interested to hear firsthand about the Jamaicans--she had been learning and reading about that in some of her conventions and journals, the scam that was preying on elders all over the country. She said that the combination of selective loss of frontal lobe decision-making capacity, together with the falling, was indicative of TIA's, the small strokes that occur randomly in localized parts of the brain. Some of the symptoms were sudden confusion, and sudden difficulty walking or standing. It wasn't Alzheimer's then, like Bud had, was Cammy's thought. Were there different approaches to working with this than with regular dementia, she asked. Even though she was a nurse, it had been a few years and she didn't feel up on the latest research. Whereupon Dr. Mary loaded her up with pamphlets and literature about various things and said that was her "homework," and that they should come back in two weeks, after they had read up on it, and things had settled into a routine. She gave them a referral to a neurologist, checked Susie's blood pressure and vitals once more, and cordially saw them out the door. She said next time they come, Susie should be fasting, so they could test for cholesterol levels with a blood draw.

When they got in the car to go back to Maggie's, Cammy had a text from Matthew: could she please come by Bud's to discuss details of Viola working at Maggie's taking care of Susie? Hmm, they were on Poplar Avenue right now, not far from Bud's. Practically speaking, it made sense to go there before taking Susie back to Maggie's. She thought perhaps they could just have a brief negotiation, maybe even in the driveway. But when she pulled into said driveway Susie, who had been rather quiet and morose, raised her head and looked around. Her face lit up, and she opened the car door and hopped out, spry as you please.

"Here we are at last!" she cried. And before Cammy could stop her, she ran to the front door and went in.

Esther was there for her shift, beginning to prepare dinner, and Bud was in the den watching TV. Cammy caught up with Susie in the living room, and held onto her tightly. She and Maggie had not discussed the possibility of Susie coming here at all--it didn't occur to them that it would ever happen. Susie was looking around in delight--all the old furnishings and familiar surroundings invoking oohs and aahs of recognition. She touched everything so lovingly.

"You brought me home!" she beamed at Cammy.

Home. This was what she meant when she kept saying she wanted to go home. The light dawned on Cammy.

"Well, um, this isn't really where we had in mind you would be staying, Mama. We think it would be better if you stayed at Maggie's."

"Nonsense. This is where I should stay--this is my home."

"The thing is, it's Bud's home really, isn't it? I mean, you left." Cammy felt uncomfortable yet oddly at ease in this difficult moment, having to lay all this out for Susie in such a black and white way, as if she were the teacher for once and Mama was her student, but what other way was there?

But even as Cammy spoke, Susie was wandering away down the hall, toward her old sewing room, the blue room.

Esther, who had heard the front door open and close twice, came out of the kitchen to see what was up and who was here. When she saw Susie, she stopped in the doorway to let her pass. Susie nodded pleasantly and continued on her way. Esther looked at Cammy.

"Tell me that's not who I think it is!" she hissed.

"How can you tell?" Cammy whispered back.

"I've seen those pictures. She may be old but she's still there in the face. And still very good-looking too, for an old lady."

"And why have I never seen those pictures??" Now it was Cammy's turn to hiss.

"I assumed you had--I mean, they had been turning up in the house all those years."

Cammy had a memory, then, of one time when she was home alone for some reason, and was rummaging around in Susie's old closet, trying on shoes that Susie had left behind. She was about sixteen. She moved on to the bathroom that served the master bedroom, and was pawing through the drawer of old makeup that no one had ever removed. There were lots of perfume samplers in there, and the whole drawer smelled divine, to her naive nose. At the very back of the drawer, taped to the bottom, was one of Mama's school pictures from that fall, just before she left them. Cammy had carefully lifted it up, the desiccated tape coming loose easily. She held it to her nose--it smelled like gardenias: Mama's favorite scent. She kept that picture hidden in a secret treasure box that she had to this day, although she had not looked at it for decades. Suddenly it all came flooding back to her, and the dam of tears she held at bay when she was sixteen sniffing that gardenia perfume burst with a vengeance. She collapsed on the couch, sobbing inconsolably.

Matthew, who was in the den with Bud, was dying to know what was going on, but Esther had poked her head around the doorway and shook it warningly. Bud, apparently, did not hear any of it.

Cammy said, wiping her nose with an old Kleenex she found in her pocket, "Show me the drawerful of pictures. I want to see them."

Esther stuck her head back around the doorway to get Matthew's attention and jerked it, meaning come here. He got up casually and sauntered out of the den into the room on the other side of the fireplace. Esther grasped his arm and said, "Your grandmamma is in the house--she went down there," pointing down the hallway. "Go keep her occupied so that Mr. B doesn't see her and she doesn't see him. I got to show your mama something."

Matthew nodded and took off in the direction of the sewing room while Esther and Cammy stealthily crept past the den into the other hallway going to the bedrooms. When Esther opened the drawer with the pictures, Cammy of course knew that drawer--it was his sock drawer. She guessed she had not known that the pictures were in there--being flat, they didn't take up much room, and the drawer was sort of at her eye level, so she usually just reached in to grab a pair of socks if she needed to help Bud get dressed. The sock supply never got low enough to allow the pictures to show. Esther dumped the contents of the drawer out on Bud's bed, and they shoved the socks aside. There they were--dozens of pictures of Susie--her schoolteacher photos, wallet size, and a couple of 5x7's that she had never sent to her mother or Bud's mother. Yellowed with age, creased, powdery, torn on the edges, they each had a story to tell about where they had been secreted away and how they were found. Cammy realized she would never know all their stories, but it didn't matter. The idea behind the action was the important thing. Clearly Susie wanted to be remembered. Cammy gazed at the portraits. They showed a vibrant attractive woman in the prime of life, firm in her beliefs and aspirations. You would never guess that marital discord lurking beneath the surface was about to change her life, though at the time the picture was taken she was already planning her fateful action.

Chapter Forty-four

Fall 1960

Maggie was in Mama's class this year. It was kind of strange, having your mother for your teacher, because you got to see a whole side to her that you never knew existed. Maggie had seen a lot of strife in her household, along with the good times; she knew Mama could be angry, pouty, and vengeful at times. But in the classroom, she was none of that, only calm and serene and cheerful. That's why she was able to be demanding and strict and yet beloved by her students. If anyone did step out of line, she quietly took them aside, out into the hall and had a few words with them, and that was the end of it. Of course in those days there wasn't much misbehaving. So Maggie liked going to school this year--it was a safe haven; she didn't feel like she had to walk on eggshells to avoid upsetting anyone. And of course if she needed extra help on something, the teacher was right there at her fingertips every night.

Cammy was in sixth grade this year, the last year of elementary school--next year she would go to junior high. She was in the "too cool to interact with the little sister" phase. Even their doll play together--the best thing they had going--had fallen away. Cammy had already "flown up" to Camp Fire Girls, but Maggie was still a Bluebird, so they no longer had that group in common. Maggie played horses with her neighbor friend, Cammy talked on the phone a lot with her friends, and the sisters didn't have much interaction.

Both girls were, though, excited about the New York trip. It was always a good time, and Daddy treated them to lots of special New York activities--the Museum of Natural History, the Empire State Building, the Statue of Liberty, as well as the live airing of the Howdy Doody Show--all followed by meals at famous restaurants, or just from the hot dog and pretzel vendors on the street. And of course this year the added attraction of "Bye Bye Birdie" on Broadway! By their now established tradition, the Howdy Doody airing was the last thing on their agenda, the culmination, on Cammy's birthday. But this year the airing was held on the 24th, the day before her birthday. They would fly back to Memphis on her birthday. Daddy had been hinting around that there was a big surprise to be announced in the show, but nobody knew what it would be. It was too bad Mama was never there with them, but they always called her and talked to her at least.

Mama seemed unusually distracted in the days before they left. In retrospect, Cammy would say that they should have seen it coming, because of the letters.

The first days of the trip were wonderful as usual. "Bye-Bye Birdie" had been fabulous for Cammy, and then they took the horse-drawn carriage tour around Central Park, which Maggie swooned at. Then came the last day, and the studio show. This is how Wikipedia describes that episode of Howdy Doody (Cammy has looked it up):

Final episode [edit]

The final episode, "Clarabell's Big Surprise," was broadcast on September 24, 1960. The hour-long episode was mostly a fond look back at all the highlights of the show's past. Meanwhile, in the midst of it all, Clarabell has what he calls a "big surprise." The rest of the cast attempts to find out the surprise throughout the entire show, with only Mayor Phineas T. Bluster succeeding, and promising to keep it a secret. ("But," he says upon leaving, "it's not gonna be easy to keep a secret like *this*!")

Finally, in the closing moments, the surprise was disclosed through pantomime to Buffalo Bob and Howdy Doody; as it turned out, Clarabell the mute clown actually could talk. Amazed, Bob frantically told Clarabell to prove it, as this was his last chance. An ominous drum roll began as Clarabell faced the camera as it came in for an extreme closeup. His lips quivered as the drum roll continued. When it stopped, Clarabell simply said softly, "Goodbye, kids." A tear could be seen in his right eye as the picture faded to black.

That was the surprise--the show ended just like that. Canceled by NBC after thirteen years. There was a stunned silence as the cameras stopped rolling, and the puppeteers put down their charges and quietly walked off set. The producer came out and spoke to the Peanut Gallery audience, thanking them for being loyal supporters for the duration of the show. Some kids started crying, some parents were shocked and murmuring amongst themselves, but most just stood up and shuffled out of the studio as directed by the ushers.

Maggie and Cammy and Daddy took a cab back to the Holiday Inn where they were staying. The girls had not much appetite after that, but Daddy insisted he was going out to pick up something they could eat--maybe a hamburger and a milkshake for each of them, and told them to make their call to Mama while he was gone. He told them to lock the door and don't let anyone in, and he would be right back. Cammy had already started babysitting a little around the neighborhood, and was insulted that he would think twice about leaving them alone, but she was too affected by the sadness of the shocking last show to argue about it. He left and she dialed the phone. It rang and rang but there was no one home to answer it. Maggie started to cry then, and Cammy could not keep from joining her. They laid on their bed holding each other and sniffling, not really sure why, but there was a great sorrow in the air somehow.

The reason no one answered the phone at the Bensons' house that evening was simple: Susie was in Nova Scotia.

She had not heard from Don for a week, ever since he and his family had left for Cape Breton. Delores had been feeling strong enough, finally, to go, so they jumped on it. Susie was glad for them. And then one day after school, Susie was in her classroom grading papers and tidying up when another teacher, who had been in the teacher's lounge when the phone rang, came to inform her that she had a call. She jumped out of her chair and ran to the lounge. "Hello?" she said, knowing it could only be one person. "Don? How are you? What's happening? Where are you?"

"I'm back home." His voice sounded husky, as if he had been crying. But Don was a glass-half-full/carry on cheerfully kind of person (while at the same time complaining). "Delores is in Londonderry at her parents' house. She got that far--we had a wonderful trip--but then on the first day in Londonderry she collapsed, and there she lies."

"Oh no!" cried Susie. "Oh Don (she almost called him 'honey' but stopped herself)--I'm so sorry! Who has the children?"

"Well I do, and it's hard because I'm kind of trying to work a little bit too, although it doesn't seem like I should, does it? Shouldn't I be totally focused on my wife who's dying? Why do I feel so compelled to maintain close ties with my classroom?" Don was clearly distressed about this.

"Oh, I totally understand," Susie agreed. "Teaching is more than just a job--it's a whole set of relationships, a whole little world really, a miniature cosmos. So no wonder you want to continue to be in that."

"Delores' parents think I'm a monster for leaving her there and coming back here to work, even if I did take the boys. I'll have to go up there next weekend. The doctors don't know how long she might last, and of course it's not her own doctor up there. What I should do is bring her back here. But I don't know. Am I being derelict in my duty?"

Susie was caught by that question. She actually kind of thought he was, but she didn't want to say that. I mean, come on. If your spouse dying is not a legitimate reason to not go to work, then what is? So why was she afraid to say that to him? She suddenly wanted to meet him in person, to know what really motivated this guy to want to teach so badly as to abandon his dying wife. In that second, she made a plan to get on a plane and go up there and surprise him. Bud and the girls had already been gone for three days, so she wouldn't have that long, but she would do it. She knew exactly where to find him, because of letter writing, and the school project information.

"Don, you do what you have to do. Listen, I can't talk more right now, but call me here tomorrow, okay?" Because tomorrow he wouldn't need to call her--she would be there. She hung up, and then went down to talk to the secretary about getting a substitute for her for the next several days. She would have to stay very late making exhaustive lesson plans. After all, she wanted her own little cosmos to run smoothly and on course while she was gone.

Don was giving his class their spelling test when she slipped into the back of the room. The word was 'surprise.' Don knew instantly it was her, even though he had never seen her, only talked to her. The hairs on the back of his neck stood up and his spine tingled. "I have just had the biggest surprise of my life" he said as the example sentence, his eyes fixed on Susie. And every other sentence to illustrate the words after that alluded to her entrance or presence in his life, although she was the only one who realized this--the students were focused on spelling the word, not the emotional nuances of their teacher's voice. When the test was over, the recess bell rang, and then they were alone. She was so lovely, he thought. Angelic, really. Perhaps she was here to rescue him. Because the truth about why Don preferred to leave Delores at her parents' was that he was afraid. Afraid to face death, to see what it looked like up close.

Chapter Forty-five

Susie had found her old sewing room, the blue room. It was still intact exactly as she had left it, having been cleaned and dusted regularly by the housekeeper that Cammy had engaged for Bud, once she realized that he wasn't meeting basic standards of hygiene in his old age. She was gazing around in delight, lying on the bed, opening all the drawers, sitting in the rocker, and looking out the window--she could see the back porch! She was headed out the door when Matthew almost bumped into her.

"Hi Grandma! Imagine seeing you here!" he said heartily. She looked at him, puzzled as to who he was. "I'm Matthew, your grandson. Remember, we were out at Aunt Maggie's--was it just yesterday? Me and Viola. Remember?"

Susie didn't answer his question. "I want to go out to that screened-in porch. Can you show me how to get there? This house is confusing." So he took her arm and guided her toward the kitchen, which had a back door connecting to the porch. They went out and sat on the swing. She gave a push with her feet and they began to rock a little. She had her eyes closed and seemed to be lost in a reverie. "This is where I read *Winnie the Pooh* to them," she murmured.

When her eyes fluttered open, she noticed the sunken

structure in the yard. She got up and stood by the screen wall, staring at it, then slowly walked out the door and down to it. Matthew followed her out. When she got close enough to see what it was--the glass window walls, the gravel floor inside, the potting shelves and sink--she cocked her head and furrowed her brow, trying to reconcile the conflicting memories of this place. She could not, and it exhausted her to keep trying. She became disoriented and agitated, and Matthew had to escort her back into the house to find Cammy. He had asked his mom to come to talk about employing Viola, after all. He finally found her, in Bud's bedroom, but when Cammy saw what kind of state Susie was in, she told Matthew she had to get her back to Maggie's and settled down right away--they would discuss Viola tomorrow. Cammy quickly swept the old school portraits back into the drawer, but not before Susie caught a glimpse of them, and then glanced around and recognized the room. However, she allowed herself to be led out of the house and back to the car without protesting.

When Matthew went back into the den to sit with Bud, Bud said, "Who was that old lady you were with in the backyard?" as he had happened to look out the window when they were out by the greenhouse.

"Oh, um..." Matthew wasn't sure what to say. He had gathered that his mom and Esther did not want Bud to see Susie, so it seemed safest to simply lie. "Oh, that was just someone Mama brought over to look at your greenhouse. I forget her name."

Chapter Forty-six

Fall 1960

"Susie--it must be you." Don had taken her hands so naturally, and was gazing at her with rapture and amazement in his eyes while the students were out to recess. "I can't believe you would do this for me. Have you, I mean, do you, have you made plans for accommodations?"

Susie looked somewhat abashed. "No," was all she said, looking him in the eye. "Where do you recommend?" There, ball in his court.

"You know, this isn't a good time for us to talk--the kids will be back in any minute. Let's talk after school. If you can hang around...?" To which she raised her eyebrows and spread her hands, meaning 'where else would I have to go?' And Don felt so foolish, because of course she had nowhere else to go.

"Where are your children?" she asked, and he knew she meant Ted and Michael.

"A couple different neighbors kindly offered to take care of them while I teach. I don't have to go home right away." And with that, the bell rang and the third graders came tumbling in from recess.

When school ended, they sat at a circular table in his classroom and looked at each other. He was still in disbelief that she had come, and she was trying to get a fix on who he was. She had watched him teach the rest of the day after recess, and was impressed with the easy way he had with the students. They apparently loved him in return and gave him their best, mostly. Susie could identify with that; and though her personal style was a little more formal than his, they were equals in their profession. She decided to say something about the lesson and compliment him on his handling of it. After the pleasantries of this and that were taken care of, they were back to the elephant in the room question--where would she stay? He really should be getting back to his kids. He cleared his throat. He was finding it hard to breathe. She was so beautiful--he had not expected that. Since Delores had been ill and undergoing treatment for quite a few months now, they had not been intimate at all. She had lost her hair and been so fatigued all the time that she lost whatever of her original lustre she still had after having two babies, and Don just shut down that part of his marriage that made all the dreary parts bearable. Suddenly here was this lovely creature who had traveled a very long way to see him, to be with him. He could not comprehend what it all meant. He was pretty sure that some sort of sin might be liable to occur, and this troubled him, as a Catholic. Yet he was drawn irresistibly toward it.

"Listen, we do have an extra bedroom in the house. I mean, if you really intend to help out around the place--but you don't have to, really! We're fine. I mean, I have to figure out what to do with the kids every day, and they're fussy and clingy because they want their mama and they don't know what's going on. It's hard... dealing with them, knowing what to say or not say," and an unexpected sob escaped him. He put his head in his hands then and pressed his eyes. "It's hard." Don looked a little like Al Pacino, only thirty pounds heavier. Right now he had the drawn, haggard look of Pacino's face in one of his police dramas. He looked at her with such vulnerability that Susie's heart sank. She knew she was about to change her whole life for this man. Bud never looked at her with any weakness or need--he was always the one in charge, at least in his mind. She liked the feeling that here was a man that really needed her.

"Why don't I watch the children while you come to work? I remember how to be a parent to kids that age," which was a teeny white lie, because it was already kind of a blurry time in her mind. "That way they can be in their own home, and at least that will be comforting and familiar to them. Kids get scared when they have to stay with other people without understanding why."

Don nodded slowly, agreeing with her. "Of course, there is the other problem of bringing Delores here. Then it becomes difficult to explain."

"I want to do whatever it takes to help you. I can stay at a hotel if that's better. But I don't have a car--I took a cab here. My suitcase is out in the hall."

Don stood up, held out his hand to Susie to help her up from the little chair, and felt a bit dizzy at what he was about to do. He drew her to him and kissed her on the lips. They were both shocked ostensibly, but hadn't they each felt deep in their hearts this was coming? That kiss seemed to seal something in both of their hearts, making all that came after a foregone conclusion. It was just a single, chaste kiss, yet it changed everything.

They got in Don's car and drove to his house--a rustic bungalow, Susie would have called it. At least compared to all the brick homes in Memphis, it seemed more like a log cabin, although it wasn't. It was just a dark, wood shingled house which, upon closer inspection, had lots of nice features--an entryway with a bench to sit on to take off shoes or boots, and a rack to hang a coat on while it dries, a good-sized kitchen with lots of cupboards, big fireplace in the living room, a sun porch with shelves for starting plants, a large shop in the back, three bedrooms and two baths. Only a couple of miles from the school.

Don put Susie in the one spare bedroom that they had--so far the boys were sharing a room. Then they sat down to plan what they would tell Ted and Michael about who she was. Don thought it best if they pretended that she was an old friend of Delores, come to help out in her last days. Susie agreed to that, although with slight misgivings. Then he called Londonderry, to Delores' parents, to get the daily report of how she was doing. It seemed she was going downhill fast. He told them he would call back in a little while. He walked over to the neighbor's house to retrieve the boys, who were hungry and needy; Michael had green snot running down his lip. Susie meanwhile looked in the refrigerator to see what she might fix for dinner. It was filled with dishes of food that friends and neighbors had brought over--casseroles, soups, stews, cakes and pies. Goodness, she wouldn't have to cook at all. She wandered around until she found the washer and dryer, and some dirty clothes. Ah--she knew what to do with those. She watered houseplants that were thirsty, dusted the wooden furniture and the window sills, and took out the garbage. When Don got back with the children, she had put some cookies out on a plate for them, with a glass of milk for each. They were introduced and the boys accepted her presence in their home as just another circumstance they would have to get used to. They were pretty well-behaved guys, she had to give someone credit for that. After a meal and a bath they were put to bed, then Susie and Don were left to discuss the situation.

"I think you should go up there, go to her. Stay there until the end--it can't be far off. You need to do that, Don." Susie was, as always, opinionated, and had good arguments to back up her opinions. This wasn't a hard one because Don actually knew in his soul that he should go and be with Delores. Reluctantly he called the school secretary and told her to arrange for a substitute for an indefinite number of days, or perhaps weeks. She understood and said she had the perfect person in mind. Then he called his in-laws back and told them he would be up tomorrow morning before noon, and he intended to stay there until the end. They were relieved and happy to hear that he had some help with the boys, though he was vague about that part with them, not saying that it was an old friend of Delores, but a colleague of his. Which was true, in a way.

Even though it had only been several days since he had seen her, Don was shocked by Delores' appearance.

She seemed to have shrunk to half her size. Her skin was powdery dry and white, her eyes were sunken in. He found it hard to look, but he forced himself to do it. He sat by the bed holding her hand and squeezing a little sponge of water onto her lips once in a while. She floated in and out of consciousness. He had gotten there none too soon--she left her body late that very night. He was able to say goodbye, and how much he loved her, and all that he needed to say. Promised her he would take good care of the boys, and then sat vigil until it was over. He felt exhausted but proud of himself for doing it. For which he gave Susie all the credit. What if she had not come? He would not have been here for the end. He would have blamed himself for that for the rest of his life. Susie was a miracle.

And so it happened that Susie was embroiled in the death of a woman she never met, two thousand miles away, and was not at home when her daughter called from New York to share birthday news.

Chapter Forty-seven

Susie was back at Maggie's. The new problem now--because, as Maggie was beginning to realize, it was all just going to be a series of problems from here on out--was that Susie was miserable. She cried constantly, pleading "Take me home." It didn't take long for Maggie to get tired of that. Her first move was to call in Cammy of course, who came over right away. They made another appointment with the gerontologist. They recruited Esther to come over and work her magic skills on Susie. They made more mixtapes of music they thought might bring on some lucidity, if only for a little while. They still had to work on those pesky end-of-life directives and the whole will thing, if there was one. Maggie had the realization one day that they should call the Canadians and ask them about some of this stuff--had they not ever addressed these issues? Did they neglect to tell them anything?

"I mean, when you think about it, she was really their mom for almost their whole lives--they probably don't even remember their real mom. She was their mom longer than she was our mom, way longer," Maggie said to Cammy, with a wondering tone. "And then they just pawn her off on us when the going gets rough?"

"If you recall, you were the one begging me to say yes to this, and also because of Mama's pleading," Cammy pointed out. "And yes, Meghan and Anne made it pretty clear they wanted no part in taking care of her, so I guess Ted and Michael are too pussy-whipped to object."

As if on cue, but minus the Twilight Zone music, Maggie's cell phone rang. It was Ted. "Hi there--how's it going?" came his greeting.

"As a matter of fact, Ted, it's hard. Mama keeps saying she wants to go home. And crying all the time. We are trying to figure out what to do or what she even means, and everything is quite hard. We were just sitting here discussing calling you. Wondering if you ever addressed um, end-of-life issues, a will, stuff like that, and simply forgot to mention those to us. Everything happened in such a whirlwind. Medical records also."

"Gosh, I know. After you left, that kind of thing came to mind and I wished I had thought to talk about it when you were here. Really sorry, Maggie."

"Well," said Maggie.

"Actually I was wondering if I could speak to Mom. I find I kind of miss her."

Although Maggie felt funny hearing him call Susie 'Mom,' she herself had just had that epiphany--that Susie was indeed their mom, so she had to get over it quickly. "Oh sure. Sure. Um, Ted? Do you remember any music that was popular that she would have heard or liked in her time there?"

"Do I remember any music in my lifetime, is that what you're asking me?" He laughed. "Maggie, I'm not the one with dementia." And he reeled off a list of music that they all listened to. Maggie was jotting it all down as fast as she could.

"See, we heard about this thing where music somehow revives memory in dementia patients, so we're trying that. It kinda works. We're making mixtapes to have in our arsenal. I think we might have some songs you mentioned. Let me put those on before you talk to her, okay? I'm just saying it might go better." Maggie stage whispered to Cammy, "Ray Charles. Stevie Wonder, and some Beatles." Cammy gave her the OK sign and cued them up on the CD player. She turned up the volume so Susie could hear it in the living room, where she and Esther were hanging out. Esther was so good at making conversation with dementia clients.

Sure enough, within seconds Susie was moving her body, snapping her fingers, and tapping her feet. Esther, also knowing that music of course, got up and pulled Susie to her feet and started dancing with her. The sisters let that go on for two songs, chatting with Ted in the meantime. Flower was desolate at the loss of her grandma, the boys apparently didn't care one way or the other. The house had sold at asking price, once the needed improvements had been made. There had been a small article in a local paper about Susie's departure, from the angle of the hooked rugs shops' loss of a working artist--he would send them a copy. And yes, there was a will, but no end-of-life directives. He would send the will right away.

"Mama--you have a phone call--it's Ted! Your son," Maggie choked out the last two words as she handed the phone to Susie, who took it in wonderment.

"Hello?" she quivered. And Ted proceeded to charm her and chat her up so that she was smiling and nodding and saying coherent things to him--tell Flower she missed her a lot, she was interested to see the newspaper article, etc. When she said goodbye and handed the phone back, she looked at both sisters with a contented smile. "My boys are up there, and my girls are here," and went back to Esther, who shot the sisters a 'That about sums it up' look.

Maggie then felt regret that they had not had a closer relationship with the Canadians and their mother all these many, many years. So much water under the bridge! The summers together that Susie had promised them had never materialized, and the girls were left with yet more hurt each time. "Ted? I... uh, I just wanted to say that, it's too bad we never had more chances to come up there and get to know you guys a little. That would have been nice, I think."

"Oh definitely, Maggie! We always wanted you to. She talked about you a lot, showed us pictures of you and everything. Each summer Mom would try again to negotiate with your dad to send you up, but of course he never would. He sounds like a stubborn bastard, I gotta say."

This was news to Maggie, and it hit her like a cannonball in the gut. She was speechless and felt like she couldn't breathe. In fact she handed the phone off to Cammy, who was looking at her in alarm. "Ted? What did you just say to Maggie? Never mind, I need to hang up and tend to her--she might be having a stroke or something!"

"Mags! What's wrong? Are you having a stroke?? We were having such a nice conversation--what happened??"

"Daddy... Daddy never..." a single sob burped out of her mouth and she paused to get a breath. "Daddy never told us that Mama sent for us every summer after all. We could have gone up there all those years!"

Cammy drew her lips together and took a breath in through her nose. "Ouch... but it doesn't really surprise me that much. He could be kind of a bastard sometimes. Although he could have considered us a little more instead of using us to hurt her. Did he think we hated her too?" And the ever-present featherweight pall of wistfulness for things lost settled around their shoulders once again.

Chapter Forty-eight
Fall 1960

It was a good thing Susie had come. Don had to stay in Londonderry for two days helping Delores' parents with various death details. Then when he did come home, he was a wreck, and together they had to figure out how to tell the boys and what to tell them about death, this being their first experience of it. It was all very emotional, and involved weeping, and holding, and hugging. Which turned, as so many movies would have us believe, into physical desire, which one thing led to another and Jesus Mary and Joseph this must be a sin of some kind but I can't help it. Technically, Don supposed that he was not married anymore. But what was the statute of limitations on that, after which it was okay to consort again but not before which? Surely more than three days.

Susie knew she had only a few days to be there before Bud and the girls came home, but when the dam of desire burst, she gave herself over freely to the experience. She stayed longer than she had intended, to "help Don," but also to allow the falling in love to happen. She helped Don get Delores buried in the Catholic cemetery and decipher all the legal paperwork around death, and then at night they would fall into each other's arms. Don, it turned out, was pretty amenable to suggestion in the lovemaking department, despite grieving intensely.

And so it happened that, in addition to her not being home when Cammy called her that night, she was not even home when they returned from New York. They walked into an empty dark house with no note of explanation, no nothing. It felt like the fadeout of the Howdy Doody Show times fifty. Bud massaged his forehead a lot. He hadn't been able to confirm with her their flight information on the phone the night she didn't answer, so perhaps that explained why she hadn't met them at the airport. The girls were disappointed, but thought riding in a cab was fun too, although Cammy had a feeling of dread in the pit of her stomach. When they discovered she wasn't even home, a general feeling of worry set in that overlaid every other thing they did. Bud called everyone he could think of that might know where she could be. He debated calling the police to file a missing person report but before he could do that, Susie called them.

"Susie? Oh thank God--where are you???"

"I am visiting a friend who just lost their spouse--it's pretty far away, and I stayed longer than I meant to. Sorry." Susie was impersonal, and noncommittal about when she might return. Bud had really no choice but to accept her explanation and adapt to the situation. Maggie had to return to school--her mother's class!--without knowing why her mother wasn't there or where she was. That was traumatic for Maggie. Everyone looked at her strangely when she could not answer their questions. Miss Holloway, the substitute, in particular looked at her with horrified pity.

In the end it was Miss Holloway's notice to the school that she was unable to continue past the dates arranged by Mrs. Benson, due to some personal business of her own, and the school's inability to notify Susie, which resulted in another substitute being engaged, and no lesson plans in place, that drove Susie back home. She had called home again, and this time talked to the girls, and Maggie wailed and wailed, and went on about the terrible situation in her classroom, the new substitute that had no plans or control. Susie decided instantly to go back the next day and put things to right. Although how she thought to put her marriage to right was a weighty knot in her chest. She and Don spent one last glorious night together, and then she left him to deal with being a widower with two small children and a full-time career. He pleaded with her to come back to him--he needed her! She gave him her home phone number.

Susie could not have said when exactly she knew that she was going back to live with Don. It just seemed inevitable to her by the time she got home to Memphis. Things were awkward at home; Bud was suspicious of her story and wanted more explanation, largely due to Cammy having told him about the letters. She could not resist tattling on her mother, in hopes that someone could stop whatever was happening. Susie was evasive and impatient to get back to her classroom. Decisive action was needed. She wished Connie was still here for consultation. What would Connie have advised, she wondered, and suddenly she knew. She called Don.

"Could I get a job at your school?"

Don was worn out from grieving and parenting and teaching, and wanted nothing more than for her to come back. He was overjoyed to hear her question, and gave her the information she needed to submit her application and credentials. In fact he thought there might be an opening as one teacher was pregnant and going on maternity leave.

Susie started staying very late at school, doing all her planning, bringing nothing home, and also talking to Don from the teacher's lounge phone. Filling out all the forms for the application to the school district in Nova Scotia. Nova Scotia! She could hardly bring herself to face what she was doing here. When she was at home with the family, she was very huggy with the girls, just coming and sitting next to them and cuddling, gazing out into the middle distance, saying nothing. This confused and worried them more than any of her behavior so far. They endured it stoically, sitting very still, hardly breathing, but secretly reveling in the touch and the cuddling they hadn't had much of recently, even if they were ten and twelve years old.

Chapter Forty-nine

Inexplicably, Bud has been heard whistling lately, whereas that was never much of a thing that he did. And the tune he is whistling is "Susie Q." Matthew has seen him do this a couple of times now. He took note of it, as did Esther, who after all, had seen Susie in the house, and who definitely raised an eyebrow when she heard the whistling. Viola had also heard it, though she didn't know the song, so she had no reason to think twice about it.

The next doctor's appointment rolled around very soon, time marching on as it does, and this was the one where Susie had fasted preceding a blood draw. That was followed by a lengthy interview with the doctor where it was all explained--the TIA's causing the temporary frontal lobe impairment, the falling--Susie had had one fall so far at Maggie's--and Cammy hoped that Susie was taking it all in. However, what actually was happening was she was having a TIA while the doctor was talking. She began a rambling time-traveling line of conversation that cut short the session. Cammy whisked her away to get some food in her, believing that low blood sugar might affect the condition, though the doctor assured her it did not. What do they really know, thought Cammy, as she packed Susie into the car and drove to Bud's as fast as she could because she knew there would be food at the house they could have, and it was close. She figured Susie had already been inside once and they kept Bud from seeing her (so she thought), so they could do it again.

This time Susie did not react when they drove into the driveway of her "home." Cammy got her out of the car and they walked slowly up the walk to the door, Cammy holding Susie's elbow lest she fall again. She opened the door quietly and led Susie to the couch to sit down while she checked on where everybody was. The coast was clear--no one was even anywhere in sight. Cammy quickly assessed the refrigerator for food possibilities, and slapped together a ham and cheese and pickle sandwich as fast as she could, but when she got back to the living room Susie was gone. Once again she had wandered down the hall and found her old sewing room and was sitting in the rocking chair.

"Hello dear!" she said happily, upon seeing Cammy. "How are you? How nice to see you!"

"Oh I'm good, Mama--how about yourself? Are you hungry? I made you a sandwich."

"That sounds lovely. Thank you."

While Cammy darted back to the living room to get the sandwich, Susie gazed out the window, where in plain sight Matthew was trying to get Bud to rake some leaves that had fallen early. "Who is that old man out there?" she asked Cammy when she arrived with the sandwich.

The question caught Cammy by surprise, since she hadn't looked outside, and when she did, before she thought what she was saying she said, "Why, that's

Daddy of course," which she instantly regretted. But she had no time to think about it because her phone rang just then. It was Maggie having an emergency--she had gone to the post office to mail *A Wrinkle in Time* to the collector who was going to pay her $10,500 for it. If it passed muster with them, they would put the check in the mail in the next post. That's how the process worked--it was an honor system much like eBay--if you weren't a good player you eliminated yourself. Anyway, she had gotten in a minor fender-bender--not her fault, she hastened to assure Cammy--but her car was a mess and actually not drivable. Could Cammy come pick her up? AAA was on their way to tow hers. Also she might have a sprained collarbone or something, also maybe whiplash.

Jesus Christ, thought Cammy. Could my life get any harder? And then felt so guilty, because, of course it could. She could be a refugee fleeing Syria, or a Honduran woman trying to cross the southern border illegally through the desert.

"Okay, Mama--finish your sandwich. We have to go pick up Maggie."

"Oh no, dear--you can go all by yourself now that you have your license. I need to stay here and start dinner."

Cammy was momentarily stumped. She wasn't about to get into a battle of wills with her mother, like you would a defiant toddler. She looked out the window and rapped on it to get Matthew's attention. He looked up at her and waved; she motioned for him to come in. He glanced at Bud, told him he'd be right back, and trotted up to the back door.

"Maggie's had an accident and I need to go pick her up right now, and maybe even take her to the ER, I don't know, but she might be hurt. Or in shock. Mama won't go. Can she somehow stay here? Could you manage both of them? And could they not be in the same space? Where's Viola?"

To his credit, Matthew did not get flustered with this barrage of information and questions. He expressed concern over Maggie, and said he could handle it, and that Viola had left already but Esther would soon come for her shift, so he thought it could be done. Breathing a sigh of relief, Cammy gave him a big hug and rushed out to her car.

Maggie was all the way out in Collierville of course, so it took her a little while to get there. At first Cammy didn't see her, because the car was gone--AAA had beaten her there. Then she saw a frazzled-looking redhead with grey roots showing sitting on a bench outside a Chick Fil-A, where she had been heading to get a little bite to eat when the light turned red before she thought it would and she didn't have time to complete her left turn before some antsy driver plowed into her. Thankfully they weren't going fast at all, so the damage could have been worse, but still. Maggie was holding herself stiffly, afraid to move too suddenly. When she saw Cammy, she cried, "Oh, thank God. Take me home--I want a hot bath immediately!" Cammy gingerly inspected her sister for any broken bones. She really was inclined to take her to the ER, but Maggie was adamant that she would be fine with some ibuprofen and a good soak.

When they got to the house, Cammy half lifted her sister out of the car (an SUV with just a wee bit of a big step up) and held onto her while they made their way to the door. Once inside, she ran upstairs, well not actually but she was out of breath anyway, and drew the hottest bath she could, found the ibuprofen, made sure Maggie could undress herself, and sank down on the leather couch in the living room to catch a breath. She knew she should call Matthew and see how it was going and race back over there to retrieve Susie, but she just didn't. Instead she pulled out her phone and opened it to Candy Crush. She seemed to have a whole bunch of lives and rewards today for some reason, and she happily escaped into that world until Maggie's call roused her. "Cam? What are you doing? It's so quiet."

"Oh nothing--playing Candy Crush if you must know. I know you look down on me for doing that, but here's another life lesson I've learned. You win some, you lose some. Don't be attached. Watch them sail by, take notice, participate, observe, but don't be attached. It's very Zen." And then, brought up short by the sheer ridiculousness of her shouting Zen philosophy up the stairs into the bathroom to her sister in defense of an addiction that did indeed make millions of dollars off susceptible people, she dialed Matthew at last. "Now I'm calling Matthew though. Are you happy?" she yelled.

Chapter Fifty
Fall 1960

As soon as the letter came accepting her paperwork and credentials and extending an offer of an interview, Susie started packing. She knew she wouldn't be able to take much--two large suitcases was all she could allow herself. She gathered things from her bedroom, her desk, and a few things from the kitchen. She was in her sewing room, looking around wistfully, regretting the loss of all that. She thanked BOB for his service and left him in his drawer--she didn't think she would be needing him anymore.

The next day she submitted her resignation to the school, effective immediately, or as soon as a long-term replacement that met with her approval could be found. Miss Holloway, it turned out, was available, so that was a relief. Now to tell the class--she dreaded that more than anything. She knew she had to somehow get Maggie out of there before she told them, since her own family had not even been told yet. (Susie was somewhat of a procrastinator after all.) She took her out into the hall and pretended that she was concerned that Maggie had a fever--her face was flushed because they had just returned from recess--and insisted that she go to the school nurse and that the nurse should have her lie down and rest. Maggie was perplexed by this--normally Susie was not an overly anxious mother about such things--but had no choice other than to comply. While she was gone, Susie announced her big news--it was the last item of the day, and for her last assignment, she had them each write her a letter, saying what they hoped for themselves in the future. These she would take with her. The children were in shock and totally unable to focus on what they hoped for their future. Consequently the letters were not as coherent as Susie's high standards would have wished for, but then things sometimes work out differently than we hope. It was almost time to go. The packets of school pictures had to be passed out and sent home, as they had come in from the photography studio. Susie asked each of her students for one of their little prints that she could keep, and she gave each of them hers and signed it. So that took up all the rest of the time, and the bell was about to ring. The nurse sent Maggie back to class. Everyone stared at her when she came in. Some looks said 'We'll miss you,' as they naturally assumed that Mrs. Benson would be leaving with her family (Susie's information had been vague--she was taking another job somewhere far away), and other looks said 'Why didn't you tell us about this?', and still others were just puzzled, and a few were pitying. Those were the ones that worried Maggie. In fact she worried so much about it that she really did start to feel ill. Her sense of foreboding was more insistent than anything she had ever experienced before. They all rode home together in total silence, Cammy, of course being unaware of any of it, though she could feel the heaviness, and it transmitted itself to her.

When they got home, Susie sat them down on the couch in the living room--a clue that something important was about to go down--and gathered them close to her. Maggie thought she might throw up from anxiety. And without further ado, she told them bluntly what she was doing. There was no way to ease into it, Susie figured, so better to just dive in all at once. She was moving very far away to live with another man. Or at least that's what she assumed would happen. She was sorry for all the arguing they had endured between her and Daddy, sorry if they had felt neglected. And… things happen between grownups that sometimes make it impossible to live together even though the two did love each other.

The girls couldn't take it in. What? Surely they misunderstood her. But she had put it as plainly as she could, in third-grade words.

"But Mama--what about us? Who will take care of us?" Maggie quavered, tears filling her eyes. Susie assured them that Daddy would take very good care of them--she had total faith in Bud regarding that, and also she had contacted Mrs. Wise and arranged for her to come in the after-school hours and fix dinners, starting tomorrow. She led them down the hall and showed them her packed luggage, waiting in the sewing room.

"Girls, go to your room and give me a few minutes, please. I don't have long before my cab arrives. There's something I need to do," said Susie, her eyes also brimming. The sisters turned and stumbled away, sniffling and wiping their eyes. Susie went down the hall to her bedroom, drew a letter out of the single drawer in her night stand, and placed it on the bed on his side. She knew she was taking the coward's way, but she just couldn't face the drama that would ensue if she told him in person. Then she sat down on the bed and removed from her voluminous handbag her packet of school pictures.

Half an hour later, she knocked on the door of the girls' room. It was time for her to go. She had her coat on and both large suitcases in hand, as well as her giant purse that contained necessary paperwork, money, cosmetics, hairbrush, and other personal items.

"So, you already told Daddy you're leaving?" Cammy asked. The girls were still trying to piece together some understanding.

"Um," Susie cleared her throat, "not exactly to his face. No, girls, I'm afraid I chickened out on that one. I wrote him a letter. He hasn't seen it yet. Sorry. I'm really sorry. Girls--I love you so much. I can't believe I'm doing this! But--I am! And so off I go. I will miss you so much! We'll have the summers though!" She was backing down the front walk toward the waiting cab. She stopped and put down the luggage and held out her arms for them to run into for one last hug. They were all sobbing. The cab driver put the bags in the trunk for her and held the back door open. She gave them one long tearful look, and said, "Bye kids," then turned and got in the cab. It was exactly like Clarabell the Clown, only a thousand times worse.

Chapter Fifty-one

Matthew answered his phone. "Hi, Ma. How's Aunt Maggie?"

"She's in a hot bath, stiff but I think that's all. She refused to go to the ER. How are things there?"

"Splendid! Esther has been a rock--she's back there in the sewing room just chatting it up with Grandma. She's invited her to stay for dinner. I think we will serve Grandpa in the den and her in the kitchen, which should work."

"Wow. Nice work. I'll come get her after we have a bite to eat then. Thanks!"

Cammy went into Maggie's kitchen and made them a cozy little dinner of scrambled eggs and toast with hash browns. Maggie was feeling much better after the long hot bath and a hot toddy, and the dinner put her in an even better frame of mind. She was so relieved not to have Susie there that night--one less thing for her to worry about. Of course she was coming right back, she reminded herself. Right after they had coffee, Cammy was going to go get her. They took their coffee in the living room and put on a Nina Simone album. Maggie took out her secret stash of weed and rolled a joint and lit it. She offered it to Cammy, who, uncharacteristically, took a hit. And then another. Before long they were enjoying themselves immensely, reminiscing about old good times, and giggling to the point of almost peeing their pants recalling one incident after another during the Holiday Inn campground era.

"Oh shit!" Cammy raced away toward the bathroom, laughing and holding her crotch, which made Maggie scream with laughter. When they had both caught their breath (Cammy made it just in time) and calmed down, Cammy looked at the time.

"Oh shit again--I've got to call Matthew. Or just go over there and get Mama. What should I do, Mags? Should I call first?"

"Um, I guess you could call, in case there is some other thing that you should know before you come. These days, I try to be prepared, but this shit has been flying at us so fast, it's kind of hard to keep up. Isn't it? Or is it just me?"

Cammy agreed that the shit had indeed been coming pretty fast. As they were discussing these matters and wondering whether she should call, her phone rang. Matthew beat her to the punch.

"Hi, Ma. Just wanted to let you know that Grandma's asleep safe and sound for the night. So don't bother coming after her tonight."

"What?? Where? How?"

"Oh, Esther guided her back to the sewing room after she finished eating, and they started looking through some drawers in there and found an old nightgown of hers from way back then. It still fits her. She's snuggled in that old daybed, happy as a clam. I don't know if she has any meds that she should have taken, or what. Guess

I should have called earlier about that--sorry."

"Oh gosh. Y'know, that's okay Matt. I don't think any of them are that critical that missing one will kill her. And that's... amazing. I... huh. Okay, I'll be over in the morning then. Night. Love you." Cammy hung up and turned to Maggie. "She's spending the night. Sleeping in her blue room."

Maggie took this in, pressed her lips together, and tried to stifle another giggle but failed. Then it turned into more of a spluttering snort, and finally she gave into it altogether, rolling onto her side and shaking with laughter. Cammy joined her in this, and they spent the rest of the evening pleasantly engaged in unstressful irresponsibility. Cammy had already decided to sleep there, so as a nightcap they had a little sipping whiskey and listened to more Nina Simone before going off to a night of blissful slumber.

Chapter Fifty-two

Fall 1960

Bud came home from work to find his daughters traumatized and weeping. Unable to decipher what they were saying through their tears and hiccupping, he followed Cammy into his bedroom, where she pointed at the letter on his bed. He ripped it open, read the first two lines and sat down on the bed, weak in the knees. This could not be happening. He refused to believe it. He bellowed like an enraged bull, then considered the girls, who were already practically hysterical. He didn't want to frighten them. He gathered them in his arms, and they all sobbed together for a little while. And then, when the tears ran out, as they eventually do, came the soldiering on. Because what else is there? He said they were going out for dinner, and where would they most like to go? The sisters looked at each other. Definitely not Britling's, they knew that much. They agreed on Pete and Sam's--an old family business known for their delicious Italian food.

And thus began the unconscious utilization of their poor left-behind daughter-ness to get special treats from Daddy and others. Because of course the very next day they had to go right back to school, where everybody could then see that Mrs. Benson had indeed left her daughters behind. It was a scandal that preoccupied the local school community for about a week before the news cycle moved on. The girls felt only horrified curiosity from the other students, and pity from the grownups (they were not privy to the behind-the-back judgments and eyebrow raising and whispered gossip). Their teachers exempted them from homework for two weeks, which they took advantage of by watching oodles of television. None of their previous favorites though--no Donna Reed or Leave it to Beaver or Ozzie and Harriet--no happy, intact, two-parent two-child families having amusing little problems. They no longer identified with those people. They switched over to westerns, cartoons--the Flintstones was new this year--and adventure dramas, The Many Loves of Dobie Gillis, and, on Friday night--77 Sunset Strip, which they adored. Anything not remotely like the happy family life portrayed in so many sitcoms was what they veered toward.

Mrs. Wise arrived on the scene as Susie had said she would, and took things in hand. She at least was someone the girls could count on, and they didn't have to endure looks of pity from her. She understood that, although she did of course feel pity for them, her best course of action was to hold them accountable. They did not get a free pass just because their lot in life happened to be abandonment by their mother. Everybody has troubles. Adjust and carry on, was her motto. And so they did, all of them.

Susie, it turned out, had some adjusting of her own to do. Don was not expecting her to move in with him, as she discovered when she arrived in the small town outside Halifax. That had been a false assumption. Because he was, of course, a new widower, grieving. Also Catholic. How would it look to the community if another woman just moved right in with him? No, that was unthinkable. So, she had to find another place to live, and they began a cautious "friendship" in the eyes of the town, while secretly meeting under cover of night to relish each other. She had in fact gotten the long-term sub position at his school, filling in for the pregnant teacher, for which Don may have pulled slightly on a string he knew of. So they had an official reason to know each other, and had a strictly decorous, professional relationship at school. Their official story was that they had taken three years to get around to an intimate arrangement, but everyone in town knew the truth--it was a small enough place that not even darkness could mask what was really going on. What was going on was Susie was spending lots of time in Don's house, while still paying for her rental house. She was getting to know Ted and Michael, and practicing becoming their mother. Once in a while she spent the night there, and on those mornings they arrived at work together, though at least she was wearing different clothes (she kept a couple of changes at his house). Don tried gamely to pretend that they had simply decided to carpool, since they had discovered her house was near his (not true), but truth will out one way or another. They were bad at lying is the basic fact. When asked directly where she lived, Susie's mind went blank, and she could think of nothing but the real answer. Everybody knew where Don lived, and it was not close to what she said. But it became one of those community-wide skeletons in the closet. Being Canadians, no one said anything to their faces, ever, and all went on as if nothing was amiss, and then after a while no one even talked about it, it was just part of the town's history.

Meanwhile Susie had her divorce to negotiate and accomplish.

Chapter Fifty-three

Maggie woke up the morning following her fender-bender stiffer and sorer than the day before. She didn't know if she could face having Mama come back today--she didn't trust that she would not fall down her own self. Cammy left her soaking in another hot bath, this time with Epsom salts in it, and went to Bud's to check on Mama. Decisions--life was never without decisions these days. It was the thing Cammy was worst at, being a Libra. And now it seemed there was at least one big one a day, if not more. She longed for a break from decision-making other than what to have for breakfast and which color to back her quilt with.

She let herself in the kitchen door to find Viola and Matthew enjoying a close encounter of the physical kind--oh, nothing more than heads together smiling, chuckling over something in an affectionate way, but still. Matthew turned though, as natural as could be, with a welcoming smile. Clearly there was a development here that Cammy had missed.

"Where's Mama? And where's Daddy?" she asked. Matthew didn't think he had ever heard his mother call Bud 'Daddy' before.

"Hi, Mom. Let's see, Grandpa is still loitering in bed--he wasn't inclined to get up this morning, and I think Grandma is taking advantage of that to be in the den and watch a little TV--The Price is Right is on. We decided we could keep her busy with that since he wasn't in there. She ate a pretty good breakfast."

But when Cammy poked her head into the den to see for herself, she saw no one. She whirled around and went to the sewing room immediately--no Susie there either. Backtracked up the hall to the living room. No luck. With trepidation, she traversed the other hall, the one that went down the wing of the house where the master bedroom was, and there she found Susie, peeking around the door frame of the bedroom, looking at Bud. He was a peaceful sleeper in his old age, lying placidly in one spot, not tossing and turning. He was still a handsome sight, still had his thick head of white hair.

"Mama!" Cammy whispered. "Come back this way--we need to leave him alone." She hoped to not have to say more about who he was or answer any questions about him at all. And she was in luck--Susie followed her meekly back to the den and sat down as Cammy indicated she should. Cammy ducked back into the kitchen.

"Matt--there is no 'I think,' okay?" Cammy hissed. "You have to be sure. I found her spying on Daddy! You need to tighten up if you're going to do this job. Do you want to or not? And are you up to it? Because here's the thing: Maggie is feeling very shaky today. Do you think it could possibly work out that Mama could stay another day and night here? I can stay and help out if you want. Although it feels like I haven't been home in ages," this last she added slightly under her breath.

"We got this, Mom." Matthew and Viola were definitely acting as a unit, thought Cammy. What was up with that? "Two clients, two caregivers. Piece of cake."

Okay then, thought Cammy, and decided to take a chance on her son once again.

Chapter Fifty-four

Fall 1960 and beyond

Prudently, Susie had withdrawn a substantial amount of money from their checking account before she made her impulsive spontaneous decision to move. Because, what had she been thinking? That she could somehow work out an amicable divorce with Bud? That she would have partial custody or even occasional visitation with the girls? She had moved two thousand miles away, for God's sake. There would be no visitation trips back and forth. How could she even appear in court to get a divorce? Bud immediately closed what was left of the bank account so the checks she had taken with her were useless. A woman could not get a credit card on her own. Luckily she at least had a job that would cover a rental house, which was hard enough to get on her own. And she was able to open a bank account of her own up there, miraculously. Bud, of course, was never going to file for divorce--he wanted her to come back, period. It was up to her. Was she in some kind of trial period with Don, and might she consider going back if it didn't work out?

Having grown up privileged, in an era when women had little legal standing or identity, Susie had been shielded from the harsher realities of life. She had leapt straight from Daddy's house to her husband's house. She had never lived on her own, she realized with a shock. Of course she did spend a lot of time with Don, so she was not ever lonely, and when she wasn't with him she was tending to her teaching duties, which she took very seriously. And so the days turned into weeks, and then months, as they fell into a comfortable routine, and the question of divorce did not come up. At first Susie wrote tentative letters to the girls, attempts at being chatty, but then Bud wrote to her saying that it just upset them more, so please stop.

Once in a while she did consider going back, fleetingly. But then she saw in her mind's eye how it would really be. The girls would be clingy no doubt, or else withdrawn and sulky. Bud would be even more insufferable--John F. Kennedy had gotten the Democratic nomination and won the election, so he would be forever grousing about that, while she would hold her tongue and try not to be argumentative. And the backyard was ruined (bomb shelter). What would be the bedroom situation?? Don was just so accommodating in that department. She would go back to her job, but have no friend there anymore. Would she tell Don never to call?? That was unthinkable at this point. No, it seemed she had made her bed and was now lying in it, as her mother would have said.

The months turned into years. Eventually she and Don were officially accepted as a couple, when Don felt enough time had passed since Delores' death that it looked decent. And by that time, Susie was committed to staying it out. Don wanted to get married, so they wouldn't have to feel guilty about sleeping together, and she could move in with him and the boys. She had never felt guilty actually--that was just him, good Catholic that he was. Honestly she wasn't entirely sure she wanted to get married. She was reading the new bestseller by Betty Friedan, *The Feminine Mystique,* and was kind of enjoying being on her own. But in the end she was unable to resist the anchoring pull of her traditional upbringing. She had to engage a lawyer to file for divorce, of course. There were no do-it-yourself divorces in those days. That ate up some of her money. Good thing she could soon let go of that rental payment. Bud, of course, had lots of money to pay lawyers to delay, contest, protest, sabotage, obfuscate, and undercut her every attempt at legally exiting the marriage. And so it dragged on and on. Never had Susie imagined she would be made to feel so humiliated, so low and evil-minded. In the end, no surprise, she came away with nothing at all, no settlement for any part she may have had in Bud's rise in his career, not one penny. Because she had to admit total fault--she left him. And she was living in sin with another man, practically. Oh, Bud's lawyers did their research. Susie had to move out of her rental place into a boarding house--the legal fees ate up all her savings.

The boarding house had not been a peak experience for Susie. It was closer in to Halifax itself, and it largely housed miners, who came in from outlying areas to work in the coal mines. If it was necessary for her to eat a meal with them, she shuddered inside--they were rowdy and dirty, the whole air smelled like coal tar, and they leered at her speculatively; she could not stand living there. The wedding was held as soon as the divorce was final. Don generously paid for a dress for her to wear, as she had not brought any fancy clothes from Memphis, nor did she have any extra money at all to spend. She sent for Cammy and Maggie to come, but had to beg Bud to pay for their trip. They were excited to fly by themselves, feeling very grownup, but when they were actually there they acted aloof and superior to the Canadians they met, and showed themselves to be self-absorbed adolescent girls after all. And of course they were still very much the wronged first children carrying the sharp sting of that, which was made fresh by seeing the people that had taken their place as their mother's family.

It was an awkward interlude, that wedding, which was in the late summer of '63, just before Memphis schools were set to take in. Susie and Don opted for no honeymoon; instead Susie wanted to spend time with her daughters. She really wanted to take them shopping and buy them back-to-school clothes, and early birthday presents, and hold them close, but she couldn't ask Don to pay for all that, and she couldn't swing it herself, so they just had one dinner out at a nice restaurant before they returned to Memphis. And somehow the holding close never happened. They only stayed four days, one of which was the wedding, and there was so much going on. Delores' parents even came, to see Ted and Michael all dressed up, and because they genuinely cared about Don. To their credit, they were perfectly gracious to Susie--it wasn't her fault their daughter had gotten breast cancer and died. They were glad for Don to have another boon companion and someone to mother his boys. But Susie was very nervous about it all and seemed preoccupied much of the time. They were all secretly relieved when it was time for the girls to go back to Memphis.

Chapter Fifty-five

It had been nearly a month since Cammy and Maggie got back to Memphis with Susie in tow. In defiance of conventions as always, Susie had, between the bumbling innocence of dementia and just plain circumstance, somehow wormed her way back into her old home, and it seemed like it was working out. Maggie was so relieved not to have to be the daily caretaker that she decided to use the entire proceeds from selling *A Wrinkle in Time* (the check was in the mail!) to pay Matthew for his time. He pretty much lived at Bud's now, and was getting almost as skilled as Esther, or at least Viola, in dealing with his two demented grandparents. As far as he knew, they had seen but not recognized one another. Bud was spending more and more time in his bedroom, so they let Susie have more use of the main rooms, though they made sure to keep her in their field of vision while they went about the daily tasks of meal preparation and cleanup, laundry, and other household chores. Most of the clothes she had brought with her had made it into the house, and the family were even trying to get her started on a hooked rug project, though it was a little rocky jogging those memory pathways, since none of them had the slightest inkling how to do it.

Maggie had recovered from her collision, and gotten a new car, courtesy of good insurance, and found herself using it to visit Mama. The sisters were actually spending more time over there at the house than they ever had in their adult lives, really. They felt drawn there, irresistibly. They did this without consultation with each other--one would show up and the other would already be there. They didn't come with a lesson plan, as it were, they just came to be with her, grateful that they weren't really "in charge" of her. Kind of like if she were in a nursing home, and they would visit her there. Only this was their old family home, even better. The irony of *A Wrinkle in Time* being the thing that enabled this situation was not lost on either of the sisters. If this wasn't a wrinkle in time, then Maggie didn't know what was.

Susie seemed very content to inspect every part of the rooms she was allowed in, practically caressing pieces of furniture, pictures on the wall, objects on shelves. She discovered the old stereo, which still worked--Esther showed her how to use it, and then her muscle memory kicked in, and she found all her old favorite albums. Which was hard, since although Bud had never bought any more albums after she left, of course the girls had--there was the Ricky Nelson collection, from Cammy's Ricky Nelson phase, the Beatles, the Stones, Stevie Wonder--the endless roll of the greatest music ever, all represented in the two cabinets full of vinyl disks. But of course Susie recognized those too. After all, Canada had listened to the same things. She played it all; it seemed she couldn't get enough of music. And when the girls were there, they would dance with her. Matthew got teary-eyed whenever he watched them. At times, the sounds would drift back to the bedroom, and Bud would rouse from his increasingly distant place, and say something nearly on track to one of the caregivers, or decide to get up and get dressed for a change. Then they would have to tell whoever was with Susie that it was time to take her back down the hallway to the sewing room. That was her headquarters, and where she slept. Apparently either the house had settled, or her old bones had settled; something had shifted so that the bad mattress she had slept on but not been comfortable on before now perfectly molded to her slight frame.

In exploring that room, the blue room, Susie discovered BOB in one of the drawers. She hadn't taken BOB with her when she left, believing that she would not need it. And she had been right. But now there he was, just waiting all these years. He also still worked--she felt she should try him out once, for old times' sake. Ah yes--some things never change. Still as good as ever! But something was missing afterwards. She couldn't figure out what it was for the longest time, and then she remembered.

One night when Matthew was making his bed check rounds before hitting the sack himself, he peeked into the sewing room, and though the bed looked lain in, Susie was not in it. He checked the bathroom in that hallway--no one there. Uh oh, was this going to be one of those situations where an old person wandered away and got lost for days before someone found them? He fervently hoped not--that would not look good on his caregiver resume. He went back into the kitchen and turned on the outside light--he could see no one in the yard. He checked the living room and den--no one. He went to the front door and looked out. Nothing but a peaceful neighborhood sleeping under its streetlights. Panic set in. He did not know what to do. So he did the only thing he could think of--he called his mom.

Cammy was sleeping soundly, but the incessant ringing of the phone (they still had a land line with a very long tolerance for rings before the voicemail kicked in) woke her up. "Matt? What is it?? What's wrong??"

"Grandma's missing. She's not in her bed, and she's not anywhere. I don't want to call the police. What should we do?" Matthew's use of the word "we" caused Cammy to roll her eyes. Would he ever outgrow his dependence on her? But she did have to admit that this was a legitimate reason for him to call her even if it was midnight.

"I'll be right over," she said resignedly. Lord, please don't let this be something awful, she said to the invisible Mystery that she sometimes sent impersonal prayers winging to.

When she got there, Matt was on his phone. Uh oh--was he calling the police after all? But no, he was talking to Viola. Apparently they had fallen into the habit of speaking by phone just before they retired for the night. That was certainly a new development, but then what did she know? Still, it seemed a little strange to be doing that when he ought to be searching for Susie. He ended the call as soon as she got in the house.

"Hi Mom--I am sure glad to see you. Viola gave me an idea though--she asked if I had looked in Grandpa's room. That's the only place I didn't look."

"You said you had looked everywhere," Cammy said with annoyance. But the idea of finding Susie in Bud's room got her attention. "Let's go," she said, heading off down that hall.

They went down to the master bedroom. There was a nightlight casting the faintest orange shine into the dark room, just enough to make out the shadows of two mounded shapes, comma curves, one nestled inside the other. Spooning, Matt believed it was called. They looked at the bed, and then they looked at each other. For a long time. Cammy did not trust herself to speak. She was overwhelmed by a flood of emotions.

"What should we do?" whispered Matt.

Cammy looked at the bed again and then back at Matt. "Well, you're the caregiver. What would you do?" she said, thereby transferring the power of being the adult to her son. He studied her for another minute, then gave a slight shrug and began to hum something.

"Love is lovelier... hmm hmm hmm hmm hm hm-mmm..." Cammy's mind immediately filled in the missing words.

"How do you know that song?" she asked. He smiled a sheepish little smile.

"I may have put that Sinatra album on tonight while they both ate dinner. And um, they might have accidentally seen each other and danced together for a minute."

Cammy could only stare at him in disbelief. She shook her head and turned to go back to the den. Before he joined her, Matt pulled out his phone and snapped a picture of the scene, turned, and then followed his mom down the hall, texting as he went. Viola would still be up and she would appreciate it. On a whim, he also sent it to Maggie.

Maggie, being the night owl that she was, was still up. She noticed the text instantly when it came in, since she was on her phone--she had decided to try the Candy Crush game that Cammy was addicted to, to see if she could develop any of those virtues that Cammy claimed it fostered.

It struck with the force of a revelation. She laughed, and then she cried. And then she laughed again. And knew that she was checking off the final guidance:

"Attend to a sacred mystery."

Acknowledgments

This story arose completely out of a casual conversation with my dear friend Cynthia Golfus, who was relaying an anecdote she had heard from a friend, about a couple, long divorced and not amicably, whose children ended up caring for both of them in the same home, hoping they wouldn't ever see each other, or if they did, that they wouldn't recognize each other. And of course they did, and they didn't, and then the last thing happened. That's it. And I thought, hmmm, there's a story there. So I made up all the details, the plot and the setting and the characters, and I had a robust tale. Thank you to Cynthia.

Thanks to the four other people in my beloved writing group—Beth White, Susan Nyman, Pattie Hanmer, and Catherine Johnson, for enduring my installments, just listening and giving me their reactions one chapter at a time. I would not be writing novels if not for this group.

My favorite early reader, Marie Bradley, was the first person I asked to give it a look-see, and this was after just a few chapters were written. She wasn't too sure about it initially, since it is a radical departure from my debut novel, which she loved so much. But she graciously persisted, and read all the succeeding chapters I plied her with, and eventually came back with thumbs up, as well as some good suggestions for improvement.

Jen Huntley, another friend and a writer whose opinion I value highly, gave me some invaluable help on character development.

Thanks to Amy Huggins for informing our book group about Music Mends Minds, and all the research about the connection between music and dementia. Thanks to Margie Wetherald for an interesting presentation to our knitting group about Nova Scotia and hooked rugs, which sparked that whole hooked rug thing, though I had already written the Nova Scotia move. Thanks to Tammi Dunaway for her plan to leave her school pictures hidden all over the house on her way out, though I don't know that she actually followed through on that.

My writer friend Mark Dunn, who actually grew up in Memphis, and whose work I love, kindly read it and coached me through modifying the ending I had and making it better by letting it last a little longer. Plus he corrected me in a mistaken historical reference that I was never going to catch—my mention of a Big Mac, which did not exist in 1960. Another old friend that grew up in Memphis also kindly read it for me early on—thanks Michele Welch Barton.

Thanks to Jessika Satori for creative consulting and to Henriette Anne Klauser for general cheerleading!

And of course, my very good friend and editor extraordinaire, Nancy Morgan, aka Eagle Eye Proofreading and Editing, for her always thorough and meticulous work.

Treasured friend, fabulous painter and illustrator Will Forrester, thank you for doing the cover art, and

I apologize for it entailing at least a partial reading of something so secular you would never ordinarily even glance at it.

I hope I did not omit anyone, but that is a possibility. I enjoyed writing this novel tremendously, and hope that there may be a few universal truths hidden in it somewhere.

Rebecca Graves

CPSIA information can be obtained
at www.ICGtesting.com
Printed in the USA
JSHW051554080521
14504JS00004B/14

9 781977 231635